THE LAB GODDESS

James I. McGovern

PublishAmerica
Baltimore

© 2012 by James I. McGovern.
All rights reserved. No part of this book may be reproduced, stored in a retrieval system or transmitted in any form or by any means without the prior written permission of the publishers, except by a reviewer who may quote brief passages in a review to be printed in a newspaper, magazine or journal.

First printing

All characters in this book are fictitious, and any resemblance to real persons, living or dead, is coincidental.

PublishAmerica has allowed this work to remain exactly as the author intended, verbatim, without editorial input.

Photo used in cover art provided by Miranda Prather.

Softcover 9781462659944
PUBLISHED BY PUBLISHAMERICA, LLLP
www.publishamerica.com
Baltimore

Printed in the United States of America

To My Son

PROLOGUE

From her upstairs window, Traci peeked through the curtains at the men talking with her mother in the garden below. There were two of them, in neat dark suits, plus a driver who'd stayed with their car. Mother was relaxed, Traci saw, not quick to rebuff as she'd been with other visitors. It was necessary, of course, since Traci couldn't deal with things and Father wasn't much help. He was off with his bees just now on the furthest corner of their property.

Mother was leading them into the house. Traci flinched.

Her mother's steps ascended the stairs. At least she left them down there, Traci thought gratefully. But she sensed something inevitable.

"I think you'll want to talk with them," Mother said in the bedroom. "They have something to offer that—well, might set things right."

She glanced at a framed photo on the bureau, the face of Traci's late husband in their halcyon days. His smile exuded optimism, in contrast to his later deep despair.

"Can I talk with just one of them?" Traci gestured at her nightgown, her long hair undone. "Not up to a panel today."

"Of course," Mother answered, controlling the sympathy in her face, avoiding pity. She'd respect her daughter as a scientist whether others did or not.

The older of the men remained in the parlor, the other joining their driver outside. Traci donned a robe and put a clasp in her hair. The visitor received her amiably, rising to join hands and waiting as she made herself comfortable. Mother settled in the nearby kitchen.

"We're admirers of your and Cyril's work," the man said. "We sympathize fully with the hardships you endured. However, we think it's best to break with the past in the name of progress. The work should go on, even if not yet appreciated. The benighted will be enlightened once solid results are shown."

"But he's gone," Traci protested. "I'm the only one now."

"No, not any more. There's us. We make things possible."

Mother was in the kitchen, Father still out with the bees. But it was this trim, graying man, Traci felt, who was becoming her parent.

"You won't be alone in the work, either," he said. "We've assembled a highly skilled team in a new facility. There's ample financing."

Traci hesitated.

"There were crowds, hostility, press and government people—"

"There won't be with us. That's past. Our labs are on a small island in the Pacific, part of a nearby kingdom. A constitutional monarchy, like here, but on a much smaller scale. The island is autonomous, so there's near-perfect privacy. You'd be far from home, but with everything you need and complete freedom."

Traci looked toward the kitchen, felt her mother's silence, somehow encouraging.

"I'm at a loss. This is quite sudden."

"I understand, especially after all you've been through. And I'd like to give you plenty of time to consider. But I can't give you very much, I'm afraid, since we have investors awaiting your decision."

"Investors?"

"Yes, there are commercial interests involved. The project wouldn't be possible without them. I hope you don't mind."

"No. No, I suppose not."

He smiled.

"After all, what better to invest in than immortality?"

Traci felt the tension leave her face, then her whole body. She almost smiled herself.

"Yes," she replied, "what better indeed?"

She heard the back door closing in the kitchen. Mother was making her way toward the hives to inform Father their daughter was moving away again. Traci was resuming the controversial work that had ended her marriage and brought her back to them, damaged.

1.

Viewed from the air, the island had the shape of a chubby deep-sea fish with its jaws open. The jaws, however, were actually a gentle cove lined with near-white sand. The cove was being developed as retirement properties by a company in a distant land. Most of the rest of the island was in use by a research firm, fenced off and containing utilitarian structures. Along the northern coast, or dorsal fin of the fish, was a common area with docking facilities, while the southern coast was rocky and unusable.

At the tip of the southern end of the cove, the lower jaw of the fish, was a modern one-bedroom cottage with number 27 on the door. Its owner's address was thus "27 Cove of Dreams," the cove having been named by the developers. This would be followed by "Project Island," courtesy of the research firm, and the name of the island country about twenty miles distant. The only other house on the cove was number 1, across the water on the opposite tip, which was the model and had three bedrooms. In the semicircle between the two homes were 25 other properties, marked with little flags and waiting to be built upon.

The man who lived at number 27, Hawkins, had been on the island about three months. When he'd wanted only one bedroom, the developer was disappointed, but Hawkins had grown solitary and sought to hold down expenses. At 63, he was secure from the sale of his business but had no prospects for the future. He'd had to be financially conservative in ordering construction here. He was careful of other details as well, such as using the air conditioner sparingly. He didn't want to drain his solar cells and have to rely on the backup generator. He'd have dim lights and watery ice for a day or more.

Shooting pool one day in his game room, Hawkins felt the day's heat rising. A breeze had been wafting from the living room in front, passing through the rear screens to the outside shore of the island. Considering the air conditioner, Hawkins recalled that he hadn't visited Fong, the development's caretaker who lived in the model, for several days. It seemed a better alternative this day than starting up the air-con. Though solitary, Hawkins recognized the need for occasional human contact to avoid slipping toward insanity.

He'd grown up in a small city, or large town, on America's west coast. He'd had an older sister and younger brother, both better students than he. He wasn't good at sports except for pool, where his tall, flexible frame served him well. He'd run cross-country but lacked competitive drive, running more for the brotherhood in loneliness with other runners. He disliked crowded activities—dances, parties, concerts—but also shunned outdoor pursuits such as camping and hunting. Their complications were too much since he avoided complications in general. Issues bounced off him. He'd earned a bachelor's degree in accounting and gone to work for his father, a distributor of copper pipe fittings. He would sometimes be seeing a woman and had male friendships as well, but these things always petered out. The women eventually wanted more and the buddies moved on in some way. He never married, never served as best man. His father died and he inherited the business, doing well from the new trade agreements. His loneliness growing, he got into photography for a while and tried exotic travel. He enjoyed the trips but they had no lasting effect on his life. While not religious, he decided that he was a monk of some sort at heart, that he needed to go away and stay away from the now useless course of his life.

Hawkins looked up at the sound of a helicopter approaching over the water. Exiting onto the shaded rear patio, he watched the chopper descend and disappear behind the rise in the island, to the east. The heliport, property of the research firm, was on the opposite end of the island. It was little used until the past few weeks, with arrivals and departures now frequent and at unpredictable times. Hawkins would never benefit from it, he knew, unless he was in critical medical condition. Residents of the Cove of Dreams were limited to the water taxi for most crossings to the Kingdom, but it was fairly dependable.

Gazing past the stony outer beach, over a jade slab of sea, Hawkins reflected on his own crossings since coming here. Perhaps he should drop his prepared reasons, simply admit to anyone interested that he was going to see a friend, a special friend. It was natural, after all, for most people if not for him. And Lydia was highly appealing—had to be in her job. Yes, he was too far along in life, too secure, to worry about people knowing. And they'd see through him anyway, in time if not already. How much business could he have, after all, when everything he needed or wanted could be delivered to the island? He had up-to-date technology for ordering, as well as for other business and leisure. And he'd hardly be crossing to the Kingdom for crowds and activities, having come to this island to escape them.

Hawkins turned from the sea, returned to his game room, and racked his cue. He sensed again the rising heat, his brow sweating beneath his salt-and-pepper locks. He'd have to get a haircut when he went to see Lydia, he decided. She'd even mentioned it, suggested a barber. He'd oblige. She was a person of quality, of value to him, a promising balance to his life on the island. The balance might become necessary. He was fine so far, but he mustn't let the relationship peter out as all the others had.

He moved up to the living room, toward the front of the cottage facing the cove. The same business and trade magazines littered the coffee table as when he was in America. He recalled Lydia leafing through them on her lone visit to the island. She'd pretended to be interested and he was grateful, but she must have been bored those two days. Solitude wasn't for everyone, for hardly anyone in fact. He'd take all the magazines over to Fong today, he decided, stop the subscriptions by phone or email.

Out on the front porch, unscreened, he stood tall and gazed across the cove toward number 1, the model. Glancing to his right, he watched seabirds coast over undeveloped properties, past the fence of the research project. A project, he reflected: something new, progressive, a fresh focus for work, enthusiasm. Something that had always eluded him. He'd done what had fallen to him naturally, he'd been efficient, he'd avoided crises. He'd been happy enough until these older years, the encroaching sense of emptiness. His project of sorts had become escape, this island. But once here, he saw it was a project without purpose, so not a real project at all. It was a reflection of himself, also without purpose, perhaps non-existent in a sense. So it was fitting that he was here, away from most things, away from people, and yet he was still living, still human, still needed to get by somehow.

He went back inside to get the magazines for Fong.

2.

Hawkins walked along the beach of the cove, magazines held with one hand and sandals in the other. There was a firm pathway at the top of the sand, fronting the properties, but he savored the powdery feel under his feet. It was a return on his investment, or rather, his indulgent purchase, making it a little more *like* an investment.

He always enjoyed his conversations with Fong. The caretaker was a family man, or had been until his divorce, and could therefore relate experiences that hadn't been possible for Hawkins. Fong was partner in a mail-order pharmacy business in his homeland, but the operation had taken a downturn, so he felt pressured to take outside work. He had a teenage daughter whom he wanted to send to university. This would take extra money in addition to making up the business losses. Fong also had a son, failed as a student, who drifted from one shaky job to another. His fate was the core issue in Fong's broken marriage, so the father was especially grieved by it. He deeply needed to see his daughter succeed, to have past failures obscured by a bright future. He was grateful to the development company for hiring him and paying well. He was loyal and hard-working, seeing the company's success as vital for his own, his daughter's.

Usually, Hawkins would find Fong busy with small tasks, keeping the model in mint condition to impress potential buyers. He might also be out on the unsold properties, inspecting the ground and flag markers, or over by the dock. Today, however, he was sitting on the front porch, a full veranda on this larger house, framed by hanging pots of flowers and smoking a cigarette. His expression was somber and he hardly glanced at Hawkins as he approached, simply motioning to an empty chair beside him, woven wood with seat cushion, companion to his own. Hawkins handed over the magazines as he took a seat.

"More freebies," he said.

Fong inspected the covers and then opened one, a catalog of pipe fittings with small color photos. He turned a few pages, distracted briefly from his cigarette.

"They look like jewels," he said.

"Well, I guess they are in a way. Valuable. Value from being needed. Then for me, of course, they were my business. All I ever did."

"Yes, your business. A very fine business to be in it so long. Now you are here."

He continued to turn the pages, drawing again on his cigarette.

"Would you like a beer?"

"No, thanks. Little early for me."

"Calimansi juice?"

"Maybe just some water."

Fong left to get it and Hawkins looked out over the cove, the sea beyond. The great expanse, he thought, the emptiness between me and my previous life, all I knew and did, my business with the shiny new pipe fittings, the jewels. This emptiness: I float in it on this island, a powerless little kingdom nearby. There was something I heard about an emptiness—the great void—not really being empty, that it's really potentiality, containing everything somehow, all possibilities. Fong might know about that. But for me it's just nothing, a separation from my old life, what made me what I am. That's why I'm here. It's enough. It's what I needed though I'm not sure why.

Fong returned with the drinks, a pair of ice waters.

"Hotter than usual," he commented.

"Yeah, time to take a break from caretaking."

Fong grunted in response, gazing out over the sea. He lit another cigarette.

"Family okay?" Hawkins ventured.

Fong shrugged.

"Leti is fine, still doing well. A good student. She's happy, gets along with people. She'll be okay. As for Zing, well, you know, it stays the same. He makes a move, changes jobs, meets someone new, and it's just a new worry for me. There's no quality, no step up."

"Is he still selling phone services?"

"No, it's a time-share operation, maybe a scam. They try to sell shares that people want to dump—there's many of them now. They charge big fees upfront, even advance commissions. They keep the money even when there's no sale, which must be often. The way times are, the bad economies, who wants an item like that?"

"Yeah, the economy. Maybe it's the main problem for Zing, him and other young people. The good jobs, ones with security and advancement, just aren't there."

Fong reflected on his cigarette.

"Anyway, Leti is okay. Things will change."

They were silent awhile, Hawkins himself with no family news and Fong distracted in his thoughts. Hawkins was about to reveal a plan to visit Lydia when Fong leaned toward him confidentially. This though there was no one else in sight.

"Actually, it's hitting us here now. The company filed for bankruptcy."

Reflexively, Hawkins glanced toward the research project.

"No, not them. Us. Gaville Associates."

Hawkins took a moment to process this. The company from which he'd bought his cottage, Fong's employer, was going out of action with 25 empty properties between his place and the model. The Cove of Dreams loomed as a desolate place.

"Bankrupt? How can that be? They seemed like a solid company."

Fong shrugged.

"I don't know. I just got the call last night. The general collapse, I guess."

"What about your job? Do you get to stay awhile?"

Fong blew some smoke, ending with a dismissive flourish.

"They say I'm okay for now. Someone has to look after things. No promises, of course. Whoever takes charge will contact me. They don't know when."

Hawkins looked back toward the unsold properties.

"That's rough. But then, you might come through all right. Why should they bring in someone new when you know all the nuts and bolts?"

Fong gave a soft laugh, picked up the catalog of pipe fittings.

"Yes, and now pipes, too."

Hawkins smiled at Fong's resiliency, admired his tenacity in life's struggles. The concern for family, the eventual legacy, staying connected with people: Hawkins saw the value in these things, the intensity of living, though he didn't wish it for himself. If that meant he was empty, he'd see the void as potentiality. It was another cove of dreams, personal and private, carried around inside him.

3.

At one of the few occupied tables in the restaurant, Lydia sat opposite her client for the evening. She wore a soft gray evening gown, long hair tumbling over bare shoulders. She drew gracefully on a cigarette she held, glancing occasionally at a small box next to her companion's wine glass.

"Aren't you going to put it on?" she asked. "You've paid. You might as well get the benefits of membership."

"Later," he replied. "They know you here anyway, do they not?"

"Yes." She looked aside. "There aren't many European places here in the capital. More on the north coast, the resort area."

He said nothing, even looked at his watch. A cold fish, she thought, but an important catch. He was the head of a foreign research project on a small neighboring island. His check was in her purse. He surprised her now by lighting a cigarette and smiling through his smoke. His eyes relaxed behind his glasses.

"Will you stay in town tonight?" she asked. "The water taxi might be closed."

"I made special arrangements."

"Oh."

He glanced around the restaurant.

"I wonder, though, if we might stay in touch on a business basis. Directly, I mean, not through the ministry or the club.

Things sometimes arise—confidential, sensitive—in which a special contact can be of value."

Lydia waited but he didn't elaborate.

"I'm always ready to help," was her default answer.

"Excellent. Of course, I might also be able to assist *you*. Contacts if you travel abroad, references, and perhaps—" He gestured toward her purse with his cigarette.

Lydia hesitated, then returned his smile.

"It's always good to have friends."

"Especially when they can do things for you."

The candlelight glinted on the gray strands in his hair. He was in sync now, she thought, at ease in a controlling mode. When he worked in science he was alone, or with taciturn assistants, so he was ill at ease in social matters. But feeling connected again to his position, back in charge, everything was fine with him.

"Shall we have more wine?" she suggested.

4.

The computer screen was the only light in the room, the man before it scrolling through files he'd been sent. He was irritated, having been appointed receiver for the eighth time during his service on the state corporation commission. He was beginning to regret his legendary success, saving an old local company and the many jobs it provided. Thanks to his resulting reputation, he was now saddled with garbage like this mess before him, and it all came on top of his normal day-to-day duties. At 60, the everyday routine was plenty for Albert Groth, but he had his retirement to think of, maintaining or increasing his pay and benefit levels. He had to elicit smiles from the faces of power around him.

Of course, as Groth was well aware, there was also some vanity involved. Since childhood he'd relished the praise he received for giving answers and insights. He'd retained his general appearance since then: below average height, stocky though not fat, and owlish even when he removed his glasses. He'd typically have his chin raised a bit and lips slightly parted, as if eager to say what he knew. In high school he was casually addressed as "brown," short for "brown nose." He kept the kidding friendly by assisting these same classmates, seeing their need for him as a sort of praise. He was somehow lightly regarded by the other top students, and by teachers as well, so he suspected some sort of elitism and resented it. Yet he wanted to be elite himself, so after his bachelor's degree he went on to a master's and then a doctorate, relaxing at last as an associate professor, enjoying the adulation of undergraduates for his answers and insights.

Unfortunately for Groth, his peers and superiors still didn't appreciate him. Or maybe they found his affectations presumptuous: the goatee, the pipe-smoking, the super-casual manner. It was a small, private college, they explained, and very few were given tenure, so perhaps he should move on. Embittered, Groth relocated to a state university in another part of the country, accompanied by the former student of his who was now his wife. He'd gotten deeply involved with her during the tenure struggle, desperate as he was for relief and comfort. Now, on the larger, more urban campus, he saw her as ordinary, unattractive, and more or less in the way. She was gone by the end of the first academic year, appalled by Groth's emerging philistinism. His professed commitment to his field, Renaissance literature, was just a vehicle for self-promotion, self-gratification; his commitment to her was nil.

Groth's new colleagues seemed to sense this, too. His eagerness, his insistence on things, his need to be right and agreed with—all were met guardedly, sometimes with bemusement. He sensed that, secretly, they were seeing him like those long-ago classmates who called him "brown." He'd never pass the peer-review for tenure; he was a joke. He came to hate his field, finding it tedious and useless. Yet he wasn't done with the university, with its full benefits to him as an employee. Using his free tuition benefit, he enrolled in the university's business college and breezed to an MBA, driven by his thirst for self-promotion and praise. His teaching of Renaissance literature became quite shabby, of course, and he did no research in the field. But Groth couldn't care less; he was just hanging on for the pay until he could leave.

Assuming that private business wouldn't think much of his background, Groth applied for a state position in financial regulation. Though already in his mid-thirties, his MBA gave him a boost up the ladder to an age-appropriate level. From there it was simply a matter of resorting to his old study and work habits. He gave the job his full energies with intense attention to detail, had plenty to say at meetings, elicited feedback on his progress and prospects. He shrugged off resentment by his coworkers, catered shamelessly to higher-ups. He submitted suggestions on the official form, volunteered for work details, handled official charity collections from employees. Though not popular, he garnered a sort of respect that sustained his ambition. He stood out when there were openings for promotion, and the higher-ups trusted him. Eventually he was one of them, at a later age than some and a junior in the group, but to Groth that didn't matter. He'd been appreciated, praised; he had succeeded.

Unfortunately, he now considered, being a commissioner brought with it these occasional receiverships. The first couple had been okay, especially the one in which he'd saved the old local company, the people's jobs. The positive press, kudos in the commission and the capital—it had salved a lot of old wounds, unjust abuse from morons in his past. But his success had set him up for additional assignments; he was a "man for the job." He felt pressured. There was nothing more for him to gain; he was simply maintaining what he'd achieved until he could exit in glory and comfort. He was therefore increasingly irritated as he scrolled through materials relating to this latest assignment, perhaps his messiest.

Gaville had been steady enough at one time, he saw. They'd had modest success dealing in defunct or foreclosed farms and vacant, long-term investment land. Under new leadership they branched into housing development before the market collapsed, building on some of their vacant holdings. People bought at ballooning prices using sub-prime loans, most becoming "walkaways" once rates adjusted against large negative equities. Upscale neighborhoods became rows of shabby houses with overgrown lawns, here and there one still inhabited, an oddity in the waste. But Gaville had their profits and tried to parlay them into more, building eye-catching strip-malls along rural highways. They could offer cheaper leases in the outlying areas and expected businesses to respond well, but it didn't work out. Few units were leased and it was clear they'd misjudged somehow. Unable to sell the underused malls, they were short of capital and had to be creative, perhaps gamble, in a move to recover.

The island had been available for some time, but its remoteness had apparently made it uninteresting to developers. The seller, a glorified bureaucrat in the nearby island kingdom, was also reluctant to lower the asking price. Gaville, unable to raise sufficient capital, was directed by the official to another inquirer on the property and together they worked out a joint purchase. The resulting tenancy in common was immediately modified by an order of partition establishing the boundaries for Gaville's development, as well as for the other establishment, Essquibo Institute. The Kingdom's documents on all this were printed in ornate letters, causing Groth to squint, and were festooned with gold seals and ribbons.

"Archaic crap," Groth muttered, reminded of his years in Renaissance literature.

He was answered from the screen by another fancy document, signed by token royalty, granting the island autonomy within the Kingdom. This was followed by a more mundane "memo of agreement" between Gaville and Essquibo. Each party was to provide its own desalinization for fresh water, but Essquibo agreed to handle waste treatment and removal. Gaville, in return, would maintain the docking facilities in the common area. Not a bad trade-off, Groth reflected. They actually did something right.

His satisfaction was short-lived, however, as he viewed the status of Gaville's development: only one property sold, an odd piece at the end with a small cottage, and another sale in legal limbo awaiting his involvement. The bad economy had put the kibosh on exotic retirement, apparently. Meanwhile the expenses mounted: tribute to the Kingdom for protection against invasion, maintenance of the large model home, interest on Gaville's loans to co-purchase the island. The caretaker received a generous salary in addition to residence in the model, living expenses, and—what?—tuition reimbursement for his daughter?

Groth felt his temperature rise. He had to control himself, he thought, stay calm. There was always one best course. Just find it.

Maybe he could get this pending couple, the Hoorts, to accept the model instead of the specifications in their contract. Let the caretaker live in a tent, home-school his daughter. Or maybe this idiot in the cottage, Hawkins, would sell back and the cove could be sold as a unit for resort construction. Or maybe Essquibo would want it for expansion. Then again, why not work on someone in this silly kingdom to void the original sale?

Yes, clearly there were possibilities. Groth felt better in the darkened room. He'd straighten this mess out as he had all the others. He'd let a deputy deal with the rural malls—routine work until the Cove of Dreams was resolved. He himself would focus on the island, travel there to give it his full energies. Understanding colleagues could cover his commissioner duties. In the end they would praise his competence again, or grudgingly acknowledge it at least.

Leaning back in his chair, Groth reflected on people's jealousy, not only of his accomplishments but of the person he was. They sensed what he knew: he was a higher order of being, a kind of mental superman surrounded by yapping humanoids trying to bring him down. Fighting them off had been his life. Soon he'd retire, and he wanted to do it in triumph.

5.

Freshly bathed and powdered, Lydia fastened her dress before the mirror. She was alone in her apartment, stray sounds of daytime rising from the street below. The dress was white with a black floral pattern, flattering to her mature figure. She had wavy black hair that cascaded over her back, newly brushed, and a complexion that was fair for the islands. Even now some mistook her for a foreigner, those unfamiliar with her role in government. But the country was very small and she'd always worked, been part of the social bustle, so Lydia was familiar to most whom she encountered.

The dress fit more snugly, she noticed, than it had a few months ago. That was before she'd met Hawkins. She hadn't been eating much for a while and people thought she might be ill, but she told them no and gave other reasons. The truth was she'd been bored and when she asked herself with what the answer was with everything: her situation in life and the people in it, her country and culture, herself. It had been building a long time without her even knowing it. She'd always assumed she was accomplished and happy as could be, having worked hard early on and made moves when she should, avoided pitfalls. She'd been a good student and attended the general college, become a teacher. Through a contact, a student's parent, she'd moved to government work, having seen that a life with children was not for her. She'd avoided marriage and useless, unpromising relationships, so available in her land. She consorted only with the upper echelon, people who could help her, and she'd moved up. But as she stayed in her current and highest position for an extended time, she saw that, although she was comfortable and secure, nothing more would change and something vital was missing.

Hawkins had reminded her of a man she'd known long before, a young New Zealander. There was the same gangling frame and deferential innocence, or maybe innocent deference. But Hawkins also had the mature sense of time that she herself was developing. He saw his life with some perspective and, though maybe he'd run from it, he could offer it as a contrast, enhancement, framework for her own. She usually didn't care for Americans—the smugness, brusqueness—but Hawkins held back in a way that gave you room to be close to him. There was nothing extraordinary about him, no adventurous or noble past or great achievement. But he himself seemed conscious of this and accepted it, so he also accepted her. While he'd left his other life—needing change, seeking more of something—he saw her as part of what he sought. For Lydia, he was a dimension of relationship from beyond her life in the Kingdom, a life grown stale. She felt fresh with him.

As she took one of her hats from the pegs near the window, she glanced out at the street below. There was little midday activity in the upscale neighborhood. A scooter going by, a single peddler. She'd have to walk to the corner to flag down a tricycle. The motorized three-wheelers were the Kingdom's standard taxi service, cars being few.

Passing beneath flowers hanging on street lamps, she still felt inspired despite the day's heat. She was on her way to see him again. The tedium of the evening before, of so many other such meetings, was dispelled by her thoughts of Hawkins at the restaurant table. The duties of her post had finally yielded a special, personal reward, something beyond pay and cocktail parties, praise from pretentious men. She'd approached him as she had the others, as special assistant to the deputy trade minister. It wasn't really part of his immigration, but she was advised and was there, making contact. She'd explained the reasons for the B List, short for Best Citizens List: there were cultural projects to support, expenses of the royal family, national sports teams. There was an initiation fee, annual dues, once in a while a special collection—entirely voluntary. In return the member got a pin to wear, but it was more than a pin. It guaranteed "special service" when dealing with government agencies and major businesses in the Kingdom. The people in charge of things were on the B List themselves; cooperation among members was assumed.

She put a hand to her hat as the tricycle whisked along. She was in a double seat behind the driver, a canopy above her. They passed some vacant areas and shabbier neighborhoods, the ring of stores, hotels, and other businesses, then the banks and government buildings. They reentered the commercial ring where it coincided with the waterfront, eventually stopping at the Neptune's Pride restaurant, where Hawkins sat nursing an old-fashioned. They were meeting inside, rather than on the terrace, due to the day's heat.

"You look weathered," she said. "Have you been swimming a lot?"

"Some, but it's mostly from sitting around with Fong."

"Out in the wind and sun, the blowing salt?"

"Good for reflecting, having great thoughts to share."

Lydia ordered a whiskey sour.

"Well," she said, "I hope they bring some neighbors there for you soon. A caretaker and a secret project seem like very limited company."

"Ah well, there's these visits."

They exchanged smiles, Lydia taking out her cigarettes.

"Actually," Hawkins continued, "there's a thing on that. According to Fong, the company's bankrupt. Something's going on in court. So, no new neighbors for a while."

"Sorry to hear that."

"Well, seclusion has its points."

"Yes, and you have these visits."

Hawkins smiled as he studied her. Lydia wondered what he saw, how fond he was of her. Was she right about this?

"Have you thought any more about the pin?" she asked.

"Ah, the pin."

"I do have to bring it up, you know. It's the reason for our meeting—officially."

"Oh, of course. Don't want to get you in trouble. Well, let's see. Why don't we say that, believe it or not, I still need more time. I have special issues. After all, I came all this way to separate myself from things, from people, so the idea of joining, being a member, is kind of—well, it's a tough row to hoe."

"What?"

"And anyway, once I buy the pin, I lose my official reason for seeing you."

"Oh, we can arrange something else."

"I don't know. I kind of like to play it safe."

Lydia's drink arrived and they raised glasses. Cigarette smoke snaked between them.

"Mr. Ub suggested that I ask you to a party," she said. "His place next week."

"Whoa."

Ub was her superior, the deputy trade minister.

"It wouldn't be bad, really. We could leave after a short time. But if you hate the idea, couldn't stand it—"

"No, no. It's okay. Like I say, I don't want your career to suffer."

"You're sure? I don't want you to suffer, either."

Hawkins only smiled in reply. Good enough, she thought.

"We won't stay long. We'll laugh about it later. And you still won't have to buy the pin. He's not the pushy sort. Not personally, I mean. Not directly."

"That's nice, but I prefer you for my salesperson."

Lydia gave him a fond smile.

"I made a sale last night to your neighbor out there."

"What, Fong?"

"No, Dr. Kassander. From Essquibo."

"The secret project."

"Yes. I didn't pry loose any secrets, though. I have to be diplomatic."

"Hey, I don't care about them, anyway."

"You don't? Come on, now. Everyone cares about secrets. They're interesting."

"Okay, maybe a little. But how did you find him? Was he a hard sell?"

"No, not at all. He's an agreeable little man. A little shy, uncomfortable, but eager to please, get along here."

"Not like me, huh?"

Lydia winked as she smoked.

"Anyway, he wound up making a point about having to get back, like there was something he couldn't leave for long. I didn't get to know him much."

"Probably what he wanted."

"I suppose."
Hawkins picked up a menu.
"Are we going to eat today?"
"No, we'll just survive on whiskey and cigarettes."
"And," he hesitated, "on love?"
"Oh Do you see it on the menu here?"

6.

On a narrow bed in the plain, utilitarian room, an elderly man lay awake. The final check had been made for the night so he'd be undisturbed till dawn. There was another bed against the opposite wall, heavy duty and equipped with restraints, but it was unoccupied. The man could do what he wished and not be detected, satisfy the urge that had grown since the procedure.

He sat up in bed, then slipped out of the sheet and swung feet to floor. He reflected on the bed opposite. His donor hadn't required it, being dead. He wondered how they'd disposed of the body, and of his old, worn-out organs. No matter, he decided, he was on the way up now, and stood to remove his silk pajamas.

He felt the scars on his chest, minimal residue from the doctor's neat, expert work. They'd allowed for healing before introducing transgenes, the second stage of his rejuvenation. Though it was more than that, he understood. It was decades of life he would otherwise not have, and with the vitality he now felt surging.

He pulled on his navy blue swim trunks, hesitated to don his robe. It was lighter in color, would make him more visible, and the night was still warm. He left it.

Sneaking away from the unit, from the compound, he kept low until he reached the tall weeds. He stayed on the path to the heliport, then continued past the hill to the shore. The beach was narrower on this end of the island, the water much choppier than at the cove. Nevertheless, he waded in, invigorated by the water and knowledge of his action.

He started swimming when he could no longer touch bottom. There was no real pain though he was conscious of physical anomalies. More important was the difference in his mental self, the readiness and will to live as a younger man, albeit with the resources of his successful career and life. He would present a new persona, giving the lie to ageist comments overheard. The image of a panhandler in Brisbane flashed in his mind.

"Thank you so very much, old fart," the man had said, dissatisfied with his handout.

A bit off there, mate, thought the swimmer. I'm back in my prime while you're finished in the gutter. No matter, all's forgiven.

He swam parallel to the shore at first but then struck farther out. It occurred to him suddenly that he should save his strength, that he'd need just as much of it for the swim back. He tread water for a while, admiring the stars, reflecting on how all was wonderful. The coast of the island began to look inviting, its solidity offering rest. He started to swim toward it with calm, even strokes but noticed he wasn't going quite where he intended. He was moving laterally against his will to where the coast was farther away. After a time his swimming slowed, he was making no progress, and then he was underwater.

7.

Fong had felt sluggish getting up, sensing something oppressive in the pattern of the dawn. The morning light was diffuse, piercingly so, and yet opaque, the solar equivalent of wheat beer. He instinctively fumbled for a cigarette, not bothering to start the coffee maker first. As he stood now taking his first draws of the day, gazing absently through the blinds, he noticed the difference in the seabirds' flight. The circular tendency, replacing the usual quick, random passes, drew his gaze down to the shallows of the cove, where an object had washed up and lay waiting for inspection. Fong squinted out, analyzing the shape, the size. Unready though he was for more bad news, he couldn't escape the likelihood that it was a human body.

Close to midnight the night before, the phone had rung in the model home. Anxious at the thought of another misstep by his son, Fong had answered quickly. The voice on the line had babbled rapidly in English, identifying the caller as Goat or Gross or something similar, perhaps Groat. Rather than concerning Fong's son, the call was about the future of the Cove of Dreams, the caller apparently being the official in charge. Goat/Gross insisted the model be prepared for the couple whose house wasn't constructed yet, delayed as it was by the court filing. They were committed to a moving date and this would save the sale. No mention was made of where he, Fong, was to go, and he was reluctant to raise questions about his position under the influence of drinks. The caller had sounded frantic, perhaps unstable, and Fong's confidence in the future took a hit.

He walked groggily down the beach to the point nearest the body, regretting that he hadn't started the coffee maker. He glanced toward Hawkins's cabin at the far end, relieved that at least it couldn't be him in the water. The lone home owner was still in the Kingdom with his girl friend, due to return that afternoon and drop off more cigarettes at the model.

Coming to the right spot, Fong waded in.

The water was uncustomarily chill at this early hour, and dark, adding to Fong's sense of oppression. Why, he wondered, was he in this situation? A man his age, who should be settled, successful, instead having to walk through water to view a dead stranger. Without the benefit yet of breakfast, even coffee, or the touch or voice or simple presence of a loved one. Was it some wrong turn he took in life? Or an accumulation of smaller moves—a pattern, an attitude? Perhaps with Zing, his lack of solutions when the son went wrong, then the blame of his wife and his further bewilderment, his seeking refuge in business, a failed refuge and now a failed business as well. It was good he had this Hawkins to talk with, a man who'd done decently in business, who wasn't ruined by family. He gave Fong a link to sanity, some meaning to events that had brought him here, some justification.

The body was curled sideways, a hump in the shallow water. It was an elderly male clad in black or dark blue swim trunks. Though the face was partially in the sand, there were no signs of violence, so Fong could see he was Caucasian. Perhaps a vacationer in the Kingdom, out too far swimming, or maybe from a cruise ship, or a sailing mishap. Now, however, just nothing. Another who'd taken wrong turns, or maybe just one—a fatal error—and wound up here at this island. Lying inert at my feet now, thought Fong, he maybe had many friends, a loving family, a good business or professional career. Perhaps he enjoyed traveling, many other pleasures, made many right decisions until this last one. But then, maybe all that went before is what set up this final choice, this recklessness, this ignorance of his own weaknesses. Maybe all the good things finally set him up, opened the door he went through to meet me here on this island, unfortunately dead like this. I too am in a bad state, have made bad decisions to go with bad luck, but at least I stand here alive. I live as I meet this man who is dead. I am aware.

Returning to the model, Fong first started the coffee maker and then phoned the Kingdom. Though he shut the blinds, the image of the body in the water remained in his mind, so breakfast would be delayed further. He told himself he'd transferred responsibility, he needn't fear involvement, but he'd long had trouble with involvements, with extricating himself. He was the first to find the body, after all. How could he prove what he'd been doing, what he didn't do? His aloneness here made him vulnerable, sometimes desperate. Too bad Hawkins was away, but then his being here might be worse—conspiracy suspicions.

Fong's fears proved to be groundless. A police launch docked about an hour later with a trio of officers in stiffly starched uniforms. Their leader, Captain Rua, still in his twenties and inappropriately smiling, thanked Fong profusely for his quick action in calling. He eagerly led the others to the scene in question where, without regard for their neat uniforms, they made short work of recovering and bagging the body for transport. In the end, it wasn't much different from the weekly trash pickup except that police performed it.

"We will investigate," Captain Rua promised. "Please have Mr. Hawkins call if he has information. Good day, sir."

Grateful as he was to have the matter behind him, Fong didn't question the brevity of the police action. For them, he supposed, it was a common thing. Life was tenuous. When he related events to Hawkins later, however, the home owner was puzzled.

"They didn't investigate the scene, want to question me?"

"No. Seems it's up to you if you know anything."

"What about our neighbors?"

He gestured toward the research project. Fong squinted through the trees, shook his head.

"He washed up on our end. Beyond us, just the sea. It's up to them, the police, to find where he comes from."

That evening, as the red light of sunset flooded his cottage, Hawkins was restless. He could still sense Lydia's warmth, didn't mind the occasional nature of their relationship, but the body washing up lent a new perspective. How far was he himself from the fate of that man? Was he still living as if he would live forever? He needed to take things seriously, to take *something* seriously. Yet what, in the end, was there? In thinking it out he was forever piecing together fragments, missing somehow the great center, the source of the patterns our lives take. And those lives are so limited, so short in time despite vast stretches when we seem to be immobile, tied to frustrating sameness, suffocating culture. Maybe the world would have to be better somehow for him to be focused and serious enough, at least with Lydia. Or maybe it was he himself who would have to be better, but how do you change basic nature?

He decided to take a walk. Not down the beach toward Fong's abode, his usual route, but along the rocky southern coast of the island.

It was only a short distance to where the rocky shore bordered the research project. The fence was not continued down to the water, the rough coast apparently considered a sufficient barrier. Hawkins had to pick his way carefully, his gaze downward until he came to the point where the sea intruded between the larger rocks, forming a mini-archipelago. He moved inward, avoiding the water line, toward the scrubby trees and undergrowth above. The sun had dipped below the horizon, the afterglow sending a salmon shroud over the rocks in the water, their long shadows reaching back toward Hawkins. Relaxing, he looked out over the orange sea.

"Hello," came a voice.

Unsure he'd heard it, Hawkins frowned curiously as he viewed the glowing rocks, their interspersing inlets. Was it the sea lapping?

"Over here."

He looked back over his shoulder, toward the rough growth above. A figure in white was seated at the edge, legs folded to one side. She had long black hair, still striking against the dimming sky, and pale features that were lambent in the afterglow. Her eyes somehow shone as they met his stare. She smiled. Hawkins stepped closer.

"Hello," he answered.

"Do you live here, on the island?"

"Yes, several months now. Merv Hawkins."

She accepted his hand, her own very smooth and cool.

"Traci. I work in the labs."

He saw now that her garment was a lab coat. It hung loosely on her slender form.

"Guess that's all sort of hush-hush."

"Yes, hush-hush."

She looked past him toward the horizon, took a deep breath. He glanced back at the deepening colors.

"Beautiful evening," he said.

"They're all nice here, most of them."

"Been here long yourself?"

"Going on a month now. Still adjusting but—"

She looked away slightly as if distracted.

"It's nice," she finished, but didn't look back.

"Like to walk a bit?"

"Sure."

They moved off in the direction Hawkins had been taking. The ground rose toward the eastern end of the island, the hill around which the choppers flew.

"On your break now?" he asked.

"Yes, sort of. The hours are flexible."

"That's nice."

"Actually, we're always working. I mean, unless you leave the island."

She seemed to say more, mumbling, Hawkins not catching it.

"Excuse me?"

"Oh, nothing. Never mind, that's just me."

He let it go. She deftly stepped ahead over rough terrain.

"So are you retired?" she asked, turning to face him.

He paused a moment to take in her face, animated now in its paleness.

"Yeah, that's me," he said, "an old retired guy."

"Oh, now—"

She looked off again to the sea. He followed her gaze, was reminded of the body that had washed up.

"There was another old guy today, apparent drowning victim. Older than me, I guess. They fished him out of our cove."

"Today, you say?"

"Yeah. I was gone at the time but I heard about it from the caretaker."

"He was swimming?"

"I suppose. He was wearing swim trunks."

Her face settled in reflection.

"I think it's Mr. Tabor. He was a visitor here."

"Oh, I'm sorry."

"I hardly knew him. He was here on business, sort of."

"The police from the Kingdom will want to know."

"I'll inform Hans or Dr. Kassander. No need to worry about it yourself. They've maybe already been in touch. Probably they have."

Hawkins was struck by her coolness, but he shrugged it off. He didn't know the story on this, after all.

"Well, I hope it all works out all right."

They'd progressed to a rather high point, with some buildings coming into view and, near the eastern edge of the island, the heliport.

"We'd better head back now," she said. "There's the guards."

"Guards? Armed?"

"Yes, just a few. It's a *very* secret project."

They worked their way down the slope, tricky in the gathering twilight.

"Did you come here by yourself?" he asked on a pause. "Or is there family?"

"My husband died. A stroke they think, stress-related. We hadn't had children yet. That's why I'm here, I guess. This was his work, too."

"I'm sorry," Hawkins said again.

This time Traci acknowledged his sympathy, nodding, then resumed the trek downward. Hawkins occasionally heard again the murmur, or mumble, of undirected statements, but he said nothing. He waited until they were back where they'd met, then asked if she'd like to meet again. She looked around at the darkened stones, the black water.

"Maybe I can get you a visitor's pass," she said. "It wouldn't get you far, reception and the lunchroom, but it's better than nothing. Or we can just meet here, by the boulders."

"Sounds great."

They said goodbye and she passed into the small trees and shrubs atop the litter of rocks. Hawkins followed for a few steps, trying to watch her progress, but she was quickly lost to sight. He stood for a moment in isolation, assuring himself that yes, he had met a woman here tonight and it had gone well, despite no preparation. She was young and yet there was something classic about her, a level of quality that had always eluded him. The drive in himself to be separate had been weakened, he thought, but he had to be realistic. He was still living as a loner, was alone right now for the scramble back to his cottage. He'd better be careful on these rocks or there would be another body for the police boat.

He picked his way slowly toward the Cove of Dreams.

8.

In a shady corner of the hospital grounds, near a garden of aromatic flowers, Lydia sat with a supervising physician. It was mid-afternoon, but they were shielded from the worst heat and a light breeze was blowing. Water trickled before them in a small fountain.

"The autopsy will likely be perfunctory," the doctor said. "It's clear enough he drowned while swimming. I doubt we'd be doing it if he weren't a foreigner, if there weren't a tourist industry to protect."

"Yes," Lydia acknowledged, "I can appreciate that."

"Of course, it's important to *you*, the Ministry of Commerce. I too can understand."

Lydia smiled, turned from the fountain to look at him. He was about her age, but starting to look careworn.

"I'm glad of that. You've always seemed so reasonable. A really best citizen, not just a member of the club."

He briefly returned the smile.

"Thank you. But I'm a doctor and senior staff member. There are ethics that guide us, that should carry over to our lives in general."

Lydia nodded. She should come to the point, she thought. His time was limited.

"I'm sure Dr. Kassander could appreciate that."

"Who?"

"Head of the project where the drowning happened, a B List member."

"Ah, yes." He eyed her warily. "He has an interest in our autopsy?"

"Well, Mr. Tabor was his patient. I suppose he got to know him somewhat. Anyway, he's concerned, as are some others—the project, the company—that there might be unnecessary problems, embarrassment for the family, if the body is released as it was found, as it is now."

"I don't understand."

"There was something about the treatment he was receiving, how it affected his vital organs. It would be better for all if they weren't there after the autopsy, if they just went out with the medical waste. And of course, if absolute secrecy were observed."

The doctor looked at her blankly.

"Are they hazardous, these organs?"

"No."

He shrugged.

"An odd request. But from a fellow physician, obviously of stature. I suppose I can respect his judgment. Of course, there'll be expenses involved."

He glanced at her sidelong, then studied the fountain. Lydia removed an envelope from her purse and touched it to the doctor's sleeve. He moved it to an inside pocket of his jacket.

"Thank you for your understanding," Lydia said.

9.

Mr. Ub lived well outside the city proper, at an elevation, though not so far from Lydia's neighborhood. The veranda of his mansion allowed a panoramic view of the city and adjoining sea, down to the shipyard and beyond. He stood now admiring it with Hawkins at his side, the ice in their cocktails reflecting the evening light. The deputy trade minister was almost as tall as his guest, and much heavier. He wore a cummerbund and medals in keeping with his position. Lydia was with the other guests inside, having introduced Hawkins and then kept others away from him and her boss.

"So," said Mr. Ub, "why copper pipe fittings?"

"It was a family business. I took over from my father."

"No, I meant why copper. Why not a different metal? Certainly there's cheaper."

"Well, it's long-lasting, versatile, resists corrosion and pressure. But I would always point out its non-permeability. It gives the best possible protection against contaminants to a water supply. Nothing gets through—no germs, fluids, organic substances—nothing. And they can't weaken the copper in its service."

"Hm. And you made them in all shapes and sizes?"

"Oh, yes. We carried the full range of diameters and wall thicknesses, with fittings for making bends and turns in the pipe, for joining or branching the pipe, various types of couplings, slip couplings, adapters—"

"The whole shebang, we might say."

Mr. Ub showed his smile of prosperity, which Hawkins discreetly returned.

"Yes. The whole shebang."

Ub nodded, his gaze falling on the B List pin Hawkins wore on his lapel. He'd decided to give in and join shortly after his encounter with Traci on the island. It was experimental, he told himself, a test of his new impulse toward connection. The pin, a red enamel *B* topped with a crown and flanked by palm leaves, now graced the old blue blazer Hawkins had worn to funerals and traffic court back home. He hadn't explained his change of heart to Lydia, instead giving Mr. Ub's party as his reason for joining. He wanted to fit in, he'd said, and also not embarrass her by being a hold-out.

"Good to have you with us," said Ub. "A best citizen officially now."

He raised his glass and Hawkins reciprocated. They looked out over the coastline, the familiar colors of post-sunset.

"So," Ub continued, "you're retired completely now? No further connection with the industry?"

"Yes, I sold out. I don't retain any interests."

Ub nodded thoughtfully.

"That makes you the only non-commercial resident of Project Island."

"Oh? Isn't the research firm a non-profit organization?"

Ub laughed, a note of cynicism trailing.

"Hardly. Their funding is rather nebulous, but their field, immunology, touches on some of mankind's great concerns, therefore on lucrative industries. It's a long time since Dr. Salk. Any cures discovered out there will come at high prices to those who want them."

"They're developing medicines, or some sorts of cures, for profit? To hold the patents, force people or countries to pay a lot to use them?"

"Such is our modern age. Nothing is free. Not even what one might expect in the name of human decency."

"Did you have any qualms about letting them in?"

"We don't know exactly what they're working on, or of course their methods. It might all be for the best, necessary, and above-board. They can certainly progress faster than universities and socialists. They have focused management, the big money behind them."

"And their location here—just for secrecy?"

"We assume that, officially at least. To protect the eventual patents. But, as I say, we also don't know exactly what they're doing. I suppose we haven't wanted to."

And so, Hawkins thought, Essquibo finds the Kingdom accommodating, freeing them from the constraints they'd find in other places. Is this what's necessary for progress? He smiled as he thought of Gaville Associates, floundering with their development on his end of the island. The backside of the cutting edge. Yet also the catalyst to whatever's going on.

"I heard you had some contact with them," Ub continued.

Hawkins recalled Traci in the orange afterglow.

"Just a little. Met one of their workers out walking."

"Yes. She reported it to Dr. Kassander, of course."

Things get around here, Hawkins thought.

"Of course." A hesitation. "Anything new on the body that was found?"

"He was David Tabor, a visitor at the project. He apparently drowned while swimming, but the body is being held for further analysis."

"Family?"

"Essquibo is doing the contacting. He was well known to them, evidently, there on some pre-arranged business."

Hawkins caught a sudden tightness in Ub's voice.

"I wanted to ask you," the official went on, "whether you learned anything in your conversation—with the worker, I mean, on the shore. Anything about what they're doing that seemed—well, unusual. Perhaps extraordinary."

Hawkins did the mandatory reflection, but all he recalled was the pale, glowing image of Traci in the changing hues of dusk.

"No, I'm afraid not. She herself said it was all secret."

"You'll be seeing her again?"

"Probably, I think."

"I'd appreciate your letting me know whatever you learn about their methods. Specific actions, procedures. We might as well be candid with each other. We should both know what they're up to."

Hawkins didn't like the sound of this, but Ub was a big shot here.

"Sure, okay. But I'm not looking to get real involved. I'm just an old retiree, after all."

Ub laughed.

"Understood. But it could be important, Mr. Hawkins. Just so we're straight on that."

"Straight, right. But what about Dr. Kassander, the head guy? He's B List and all. Can't you just get what you want from *him*?"

Ub shifted uncomfortably.

"He wears the pin, it's true, but also the 'secret project' cloak. He's a Best Citizen as much as it suits his purpose, or rather Essquibo's. There are others no doubt, far away, with more to say in things than Dr. Kassander. But he's the one we have to deal with, and sometimes Hanssen, his engineer. They're soldiers of their company, no matter what they say to you. You cannot trust them."

"Sorry to hear that."

Ub looked in his glass, now empty, swirled the dregs of ice.

"Yes, well, you were a man of business. You can understand. Perhaps we should go for fresh drinks now."

He hesitated, however, as they were about to enter.

"By the way, there were several visas issued for people to join your community, to share in your dreams at the cove." He laughed. "They'll be arriving soon."

"Really? But there's been no more construction. Where will they live?"

Ub shrugged.

"Who knows? But one is the receiver for Gaville, so he'll be in charge. We took care of the dead body, but this receiver should handle the live ones."

They turned into the large parlor, where Hawkins caught Lydia's eye across the room. He recalled her promise to leave early, knew he wouldn't hold her to it. They'd go when she was ready, when she thought it was proper. He'd be a Best Citizen for her.

10.

 In an airliner high above the ocean, Groth reclined with his eyes closed after downing several beers. He'd peek sometimes at the couple with whom he was traveling, the Hoorts, who were across the aisle and several rows up. He didn't want to deal with them for a while, their questions and comments about the Cove of Dreams mess. The man wasn't so bad but the wife was a dingbat. Let them think he was drunk for now.

 "I must have dozed," the woman said, raising her head. Her red curls were disheveled from the long trip. "Do we have much farther?"

 "Still a couple of hours," her husband answered, "then our connection in Auckland. A small plane, no doubt." He sipped his chardonnay, its color that of his well-trimmed beard. "Then we still have a boat or hydrofoil or something after that."

 "God. You did find yourself a hideaway, Max."

 "Can't be helped, Susanna. You know that."

 She looked out her porthole.

 "I'll miss them all, the quality people. The real life."

 "It's only for a season. We'll see the house is built, settle in, then have it there for—well, our retreat in the future."

 "A refuge, you mean. *Yours*."

 Max gave her his mature, philosophic look.

"Some friction is inevitable in life. It goes with success. I take a discreet approach: withdraw for a while and let the lawyers work it out."

Susanna pouted.

"Are there things to do, anyway?"

"Of course there are. For one thing, there should be plenty of exotic birds to add to your list. Those binoculars will get a workout."

She didn't respond. Though in fact a birdwatcher, her concept of the exotic brought forth images of attractive men. She let it pass, turning her smile to the porthole.

Groth noticed them talking, hoped they'd keep each other busy. He didn't want someone hanging over him from the aisle, grilling him with questions, perhaps sensing his intent to delay their house. He had to watch the cash flow. He considered a restroom trip, decided to save it as an escape option. Settling even deeper in his seat, he lapsed into memories of his adolescence: making the old chain-net clink with a basketball, catching a pillow-like softball against his stomach. Always a dirt stain there on his shirt. Simpler times.

11.

Hans Hanssen stood atop a rise on the island, binoculars in hand. The rise wasn't as high as the hill to the south, beyond the heliport, but it gave a good view of the common area and dock, the sea beyond. Hans was awaiting the water taxi, ostensibly to pick up supplies, and had a modified tricycle in which to carry them. This would normally be a job for one of the guards, but today was different. Several new visas had been issued for people with the Cove of Dreams as their destination. Hans wanted to see them, perhaps meet them, supplement the computer data for the sake of project security. He'd prefer to be simply an engineer, as he'd been in his home country, but he understood the need for minimal staff, for secrecy, so he'd gamely undertaken this second role. There were only the four guards, after all, armed only with revolvers. The Institute didn't want to broadcast that there was something priceless here.

Catching sight of the boat, Hans took his seat on the tricycle. He was a husky man, low-browed, and could easily have passed as a regular policeman. He coasted down the slope, hardly needing to touch the gas pedal. He waited on the boardwalk as the water taxi docked.

"God " someone shouted. "What a ride "

It was a froggy-looking middle-aged man, leading the charge off the boat.

"Where's Fong?" he demanded.

"I wouldn't know, sir," Hans replied. "I'm with Essquibo."

"Oh. Well, he's supposed to be here. I'm with some people, new owners for the Cove."

"You're with the Gaville company, sir?"

"God, no. I'm its receiver."

Being addressed as God began to irritate Hans. He held out a hand to his squat new acquaintance.

"Hans Hanssen."

"Albert Groth," the receiver replied.

A tallish woman, rather spindly with curly red hair, was alighting on the pier. She gawked about wide-eyed, her open-mouthed smile greeting all she saw. Behind her, in the boat, a man was assisting the driver with luggage and packages. He also was tall, with short-cropped blond hair above a high forehead and matching short beard, well-trimmed. He had an intelligent cast to his face. Someone, Hans reflected, that he might raise a stein with.

"Wow " the woman intoned loudly, giving sound to her facial expression.

She was looking at Groth, but the receiver had spotted Fong approaching in a golf cart and paid the woman no attention. She shifted her gaze to Hans.

"Talk about absolute minimalist. Welcome home, Susanna."

Hans gave a slight smile and walked past her toward the boat. These first two were nothing, he could see. The driver was finishing with the blond man, chatting as he received a tip, but he recognized Hans and quickly attended to the supplies.

"Moving in today?" the engineer inquired.

"Yes," replied the blond man. "Will we be neighbors?"

"In a way. I work for Essquibo Institute, in the research plant up the road there. Hans Hanssen, chief engineer."

They shook hands.

"Max Hoort. I'm an engineer myself, but software. Temporarily retired."

"Giving it a try, hey? Nice to have the option."

"Well, we'll see how it goes. You've met my wife?"

"Yes, briefly. Charming lady."

Hoort nodded, saying nothing.

"Well, I'd best let you get settled. We'll be seeing each other, I'm sure. It *is* an island."

Provisions loaded, Hans rumbled back toward the compound. The group headed for the Cove of Dreams, in the opposite direction, was progressing more slowly. Hans smiled at their disorientation. They seemed harmless enough, just so none of them became a nuisance. The software man was probably competent, being able to retire here, and might be a resource in a pinch. It'd be a tough approach, though, with their security needs. Much obfuscation of purpose and methods.

He sighted Dr. Kassander walking among the buildings, stopped the tricycle. He related to his superior his impressions from the pier. The older man nodded appreciatively. He was smaller than Hans, wiry in build, his gray hair combed flat to one side.

"It's good you checked them out. Some new donors are arriving tonight on the pad."

Hans looked out toward the heliport.

"I'm getting uneasy about that. We can't keep that up long-term. The organs should be harvested off-site."

"Now, Hans. We want maximum control of the process. And optimal conditions, of course. Fresh beats canned any day. You know that."

"Yes, doctor. But people might be watching now. The Tabor incident—"

"We had a breakthrough there—or should have—putting us much closer. Then we wouldn't have to bring in more chimps, necessarily. Tabor blew it. He maladjusted, got too cocky. We can only hope—only believe—it's not inevitable."

"What about the body? The relatives must be getting anxious for a funeral."

"Our girl in the capital will handle it, bribe someone to get it released."

"The organs could still be a problem. Second autopsy or something."

"Those will 'go missing,' as they say—a small country's inefficiency. More bribe money out the window, but what can you do?"

"And the silence of the autopsy crew?"

"They know better than to blab in a place like this. Swift retribution awaits."

Hans looked out over the compound, sighing impatiently.

"Such uncertainty. Too many variables cropping up. It's a godsend we have Traci."

"There's nothing like a prototype," Kassander smiled. "There's no god involved, though. Her husband was just a man, like you and me. A scientist, yes, and a great one. Perhaps as close to God as one can get. But—"

He broke off as he and Hans locked eyes. Simultaneously, it seemed, they had sensed a new standing for themselves in relation to the universe.

"One of those off the boat," said Hans, "a clumsy fellow, kept saying 'God this' and 'God that' when addressing me. Until I put him right, of course."

After a hesitation, Kassander laughed. It was rare for him.

* * *

Rummaging in his suitcase, Max found the pouch of tobacco he'd packed. He was an occasional pipe smoker, chiefly in idle or especially busy times, and today somehow qualified as both. Susanna had located her small binoculars, handy for birdwatching and other nosiness, and was propped at the window of their bedroom, peering out. They'd been given the master bedroom of the model pending construction of their own home.

"Any interesting species?" he inquired.

"Not yet. Just garbage-eating gulls, as far as I can see."

"Well, give it time. We have plenty of it now."

He waited a moment for her to turn, perhaps say something sweet, but she was lost in her observations. He sidled out the door to light up outside. Back at the window, Susanna watched a man across the cove emerge from swimming and approach his small cottage. The man was nude. Susanna watched raptly until he disappeared inside.

Descending the stairs to the living room, Max picked up on the conversation between Groth and Fong.

"I really can't go more than a week on that," Groth was saying. "In fact, I was actually thinking just four or five days. Just time for the prefab to arrive and be ready for you to live in. I'm a state corporation commissioner. I have a whole raft of responsibilities back there. I don't work for Gaville. This is all extra for me, heaped on top of my real job. I'm not making anything here. I'm falling behind in my regular work thanks to *your* employer!"

Fong was cautious.

"I understand, Mr. Groth. I know you can't stay long. But the number of things I must deal with—seeing my daughter, my son's problems, the situation with our business—and then the travel time, considering the service I've given, the demands on me here, this location—"

Groth waved his hands impatiently. Noticing one held an unlit pipe, Max hid his own and continued toward the exit.

"Fong, this is business " the receiver emphasized. "Your company's broke and I'm here to see the ship is righted. Things can't just go on the same as always "

Groth continued as Max escaped into the breeze outside. The receiver had mentioned on the boat that he'd ease the living situation by granting Fong a short leave, with the caretaker to live outside the model on his return. The shortness of the leave had apparently become an issue. Moving from the model to a metal box couldn't have appealed to Fong, either.

Max smiled as he glanced back at their bedroom window, but Susanna wasn't there. She'd mentioned wanting a shower, so no doubt she was shedding her clothes to refresh herself. She'd been good in the end about the move, understanding that it was practical—given the legal turmoil, the financial threats—as well as something he needed to do for a while. And it *was* only temporary, though it would be nice to have this refuge for later escapes, should the need or want arise. The Kingdom and the island's autonomy provided legal insulation from the onslaught of corporate jackals.

He continued down the beach, enjoying the breeze off the cove, the sea beyond. His pipe smoke flew inland, incongruous here like Max himself. He passed the unsold properties, marked with flags and of generous sizes. Theirs was number 14, squarely at the center of the crescent-shaped coast. He'd chosen it for that reason. He wanted the direct vew of the opening to the sea, the world of intrigue and deceit beyond. A large, blocky *SOLD* sign had been pounded into the ground. Max smiled, thinking he might be the first to see it aside from

Fong, who no doubt planted it. But then, he thought, his gaze shifting to the far point of the cove, there was that hermit. Why would anyone move here to live alone? The waves constantly lapping, the sun glaring off the sea, the long stillness of the nights—haunting, one would think. A lure to some kind of craziness. But then, since he himself was here, perhaps it was just an extension of his own inclinations. He'd have to watch himself as he grew older, stay involved somehow. Looking back over his property, he considered whether additions to their home might be feasible. A sizable office and work area, a lab even. The money was there, so why not?

A group of seabirds passed noisily overhead. Max watched them fly beyond the fence and into Essquibo territory. Yes, he speculated, you could do anything in a place like this. Anything was possible.

12.

    The overhead light was harsh but Traci liked it that way, forcing her to focus hard, painfully, on Cyril's notes. Her assistant Ana was in weaker light at her microscope, observing a new set of samples and making notes. They worked well together, both of them basically living for their work now. In Ana's case, it was a welcome escape from the harsh limits of her national culture, while for Traci things were much more complicated.

    It was no longer for content that Traci pored over Cyril's notes, but out of sentiment, a need for emotional guidance, assurance that what they were doing was great. Cyril had given his life, after all, for this work recorded in his hasty, excited writing. He'd been desperate near the end, and reckless as it turned out, but what was he to do after the loss of funding? The newspapers liked to show the Animal Rights people with their signs, but Traci knew it was the Lords and Ladies in government, paranoia about the national health plan, national solvency. And lurking behind it all, that crazy fear of challenging God. But Cyril was too committed to let anything stop him, so he pressed on without adequate trials and became his own test subject. The flaws in the process were fatal to him, but he made her the beneficiary of their discovery. Now here she was, the end result for Kassander and team to bring about in others, making the process marketable.

Traci got up and went back to Ana.

"How do those look? Any progress?"

"Yes, quite stable actually."

"Think we can try them on Popeye?"

Popeye was a mature chimp in the experimental animals unit, or EAU.

"I don't know. Maybe we should compare one more batch. Hans is getting nasty about bringing animals in."

"I thought they could defend using the chimps. It's only illegal in certain countries."

"He says one thing will lead to another if people start poking around."

"Yes. Well, we don't want to rush things, anyway."

She hesitated as Cyril came to mind.

"I think I'll go visit old Popeye."

Ana laughed softly.

"Give him my best. Tell him—"

But Traci was already walking off, talking unintelligibly in a low voice. Ana was accustomed to this and gave it no thought, returning assiduously to her microscope. She was comfortable working alone, knowing she wasn't really alone, surrounded as she was by the elements of superior new life—synthetic enzymes, carrier viruses, and transgenes suspended in precise temperatures and chemical environments, awaiting their roles in the project. With people like Traci and Dr. Kassander, she was at home here and treasured her role, her escape from oppression.

Exiting the synthesis lab, Traci walked under the moon to the EAU. The moon was high and brought out the glow on her skin, the pale, porcelain quality that was a minor side effect of Cyril's perfected chromosome. Except it wasn't perfect, she reflected as she looked at her arm. This little glow might be seen as a positive, something people sought from cosmetics, but then there was that other—the run-on, like a car when it should be shut off. As if some level of thinking below the conscious insisted on expressing itself after she meant to stop talking. Perhaps here, with the expensive equipment, the many trials, her own and Cyril's case histories, they would have real perfection. Of course, there was Kassander's part to consider, the surgical replacements on older subjects. But there was no getting away from it, this combination of strategies. It was clear from the beginning that, in order for the project to exist, to be funded, it had to be designed with marketability in mind. And it was older people who would pay the price, take any risks involved. Younger people couldn't see their own deaths, thought already that they'd live forever. And yet older people have old organs, unable to support the process as her own had, so there had to be replacements. Kassander demanded optimal materials, as well as optimal conditions, for his work as well as her own, so he brought in the chimps as donors. He was succeeding, Traci had to admit, where she and Cyril could not.

Closing the door behind her, Traci walked slowly into the dim, indirect light of the EAU. She passed the cages of the new chimps, two males and a female, still curious about their new surroundings. Kassander preferred all males for the project, wanting as much consistency as possible, but perhaps the supply was dwindling. Next to them was Poobah, a mature chimp who'd served as a practice subject for Tabor's procedure. Poobah sat quietly, gazing serenely at the younger chimps, maybe feeling fraternal since youthful organs were in him. If only Tabor could have handled it as well, but his exhilaration at the change did him in. The human factor, perhaps, but then Poobah had another advantage: he was imprisoned.

She came to Popeye's cage opposite the desultory dogs. Like Poobah, he was implanted with young organs, but he lacked the genetic changes effected in Poobah and Tabor. Those changes had been made to certain individual genes significant in the aging process. Tabor had had decades added to his natural life, which he promptly threw away. While scientifically a success, the work on Tabor did not accomplish the practical mission of the project, for which Popeye would be the final stepping-stone. Like Traci, and based on Cyril's work, Popeye was to receive an artificial chromosome to effect numerous genetic alterations at once. If successful on the chimp, the procedure would then be marketable to wealthy humans seeking unlimited natural lifespans. Any problems revealed by the Popeye trial could be explained and fixed thanks to the rigid controls here, unlike the chaos in which Cyril had worked.

"Hello, Popeye," Traci said. "How are you feeling?"

The chimp stared at her mutely.

"Ready for your big day? It's almost here."

Popeye looked out toward the door, perhaps anticipating food. He was on a special regimen of nutrients and hormones to optimize chances for success, but he got treats as well to keep his spirits up. He looked quite fit to Traci, his eyes clear and coat full and shiny, his movements strong and smooth.

"Miss your buddy up there? Don't worry, you'll see him at exercise tomorrow."

The ethicists came to mind as she said this. They would hardly be satisfied that exercise, treats, and kind words were provided. And beyond this use of animals was the planned marketing to human beings, the implications for society when the procedure was utilized. Major adjustments would be necessary when some people didn't die. And where, some would ask, does God fit in? The reactions would be hostile without precedent, and world-wide. They wouldn't see at first how they wanted it for themselves, or for one they loved as she'd loved Cyril. Oh, well. The project was safe for now on this island near the Kingdom, and its finances were safe in similar places, cautiously nourished by the faceless consortium of investors.

Traci looked around for the treat box, but didn't see it.

"Sorry, Popeye. No treat today, I guess. Next time for sure."

She walked in a bit further to give the mice a glance, saw that all was well, then made her way back toward the exit. Having talked to Popeye, she could now see more clearly the change in Poobah's expression. His calm eyes gazed from his upturned face with majesty, as if knowledgeable that his was a superior fate. What would actually happen to him was uncertain. Kassander was planning to move on to supplemental strategies once their main goal was achieved, including nanotechnology, which influenced the hiring of Hans. The engineer's estimates for additional staff and capital needed, however, were formidable, so Kassander was leaning toward a try at brain transplants. A healthy, superior specimen like Poobah could be implanted with an old brain, which might then experience the world for a longer time.

Poor Poobah, thought Traci, and turned to leave the EAU.

After she was gone, the chimps settled down and Poobah collapsed into a sprawl. The dogs relaxed their alertness, the mice continuing as always. Popeye surveyed the scene, confirming Traci's conclusion that the treat box was not available. He wasn't actually disappointed. Since the change they made inside him, with its aches and odd feelings, and with the shots and new food he got, his craving for the treats had slipped away. He took them and put them in his mouth, as was his habit, but then later he took them out. He'd grind a wet treat tablet against the lock mechanism of his cage, some of it entering the lock and the rest falling into his droppings. It was a good enough adjustment, he felt, so it became another habit. He laid a hand on the lock now, gripping a bar of the door with his other hand. It had been closing with a softer and softer click. Wondering what he might hear, he tried to shake the door. Unsure if he heard a sound, he shook harder. The door swung open.

Popeye sat for a while, gaping at the opening in his cage. There should be humans in the space. Tentatively, he reached out, then swung himself forward. Yes, the aisles were clear. He swung himself out and looked around. He ambled back to the mice cages, grunted, turned away in disgust. He came back past the dogs, who eyed him incuriously. He gave a robust snort and one of them pricked up its ears. Satisfied, Popeye continued on toward the front, the cages nearest the exit. The new chimps became excited, especially the larger male, as if sensing something afoot and wanting in. Poobah showed little response, giving only a sidelong glance from his sprawling position. It was he, however, that Popeye attended to, not quite gloating but awaiting some recognition of his freedom, his superior status. None came so, disappointed, he turned away and ambled back to his cage, shutting the door with a very soft click.

He hadn't quite made it to the exit door, the latch he could open with a turn, eyed now by a smiling Poobah.

13.

Waves of heat rose from the tarmac as Fong crossed to the nondescript terminal. He could see from the wide-open doors that the air-con wasn't working. There was still some relief as he escaped the sun, but this also allowed him more of another feeling, a familiar emptiness. The joys and trials of being with his family were past again, and he was again reduced to his servile role in this foreign place. He wished especially he could see more of Leti, his daughter, but it was mostly for her that he labored here. If she couldn't get into a medical field, he thought, then perhaps pharmacy. That would tie in with the family business.

He joined a short line at the immigration desk, showed his documents. The sweating officials had been laconically stamping visas, but now there came a change in their demeanor. A list was consulted, an outdated computer checked, a guard called over.

"Please stand out of line, sir. The officer will take you to a waiting area."

"I don't understand."

"Your data tripped an alert. We must notify the national police."

Fong cooperated, not especially worrying. He'd read and heard of many such mix-ups in the enforcement of heightened security. It was easily enough straightened out. He even had the American official, Groth, out on Project Island to vouch for him.

After about half an hour, Capt. Rua arrived with a colleague.

"Well, Mr. Fong," said Rua, "how was your trip?"

"Okay until now, Captain. It seems there's been some mistake."

"Ah. Perhaps so. However, there's also been a grave development since you left. The case of Mr. Tabor, the unfortunate man you found. You recall?"

"Yes, of course."

"Of course. Well, this is rather gruesome, Mr. Fong, but his insides, you know, were missing from the body. We have an international complaint to resolve."

"His insides? Gone?"

"Yes."

"Well, I—how should I know about *that*?"

"I don't know. We simply must investigate. You see, you were the last one with Mr. Tabor—with his body, at least—before it was in official custody."

"I know nothing except I saw him there—dead—and called you out. Mr. Hawkins, who lives out there, he's a witness!"

"Yes, he came in later. But I'm afraid we must detain you, Mr. Fong, while we sort things out. There's international interest so we must show an aggressive response."

Fong protested but to no avail. Rua assured him that he'd be well treated, he'd be reunited with his luggage at the jail. The captain would personally threaten the airport staff against any pilfering.

14.

Hawkins was in the water off the south coast of Project Island. The sun was high, not the most pleasant time for a swim, but he'd wanted to escape the commotion at the Cove of Dreams. A work crew had arrived and was preparing the prefab to which Fong would be moving. It was on property 18, not as convenient for trips to the dock, but Hawkins would be a closer neighbor. The new residents in the model apparently preferred privacy, at least one of them. Hawkins had met the husband, Max, out walking in the dark, but they'd only exchanged a few words. He seemed well-educated, perhaps a bit conceited, but Hawkins sensed a commonality that had led them both to come here.

A slow, awkward swimmer, Hawkins enjoyed his greater buoyancy in salt water. He'd taken care as he passed the place he'd met Traci, its indefinite shoreline and profusion of jutting boulders. He wondered if they'd contributed to Tabor's fate. But there were currents farther out and Tabor was an old guy, and he was unmarked except for surgical scars. He'd just misjudged, taken on too much, something it wasn't in Hawkins's nature to do.

He decided to swim back.

Casually, watching the sparkles on the water's surface, he proceeded around the point on which his cottage was located.

He'd worn swim trunks today since more people were around. He preferred to get out in the cove rather than the outer shore, feel the fine sands welcoming his feet. Churning into the cove's mouth, he noticed the three men who were still occupied with the prefab. Closer, however, and maybe distracting the crew, was a red-haired swimmer even more awkward than himself. It took him a moment to know her gender since the gangly frame within the splashing could have belonged to a teenage boy. Having paused between the points, Hawkins felt obliged to approach and greet her before going ashore.

"Hi " she called. "I'm Susanna "

"Merv Hawkins," he panted as he stopped in the water.

"You must be the hermit."

"Hermit?"

"That's your place there?"

"Well, yeah, but—"

He saw she was giving someone else's assessment. Glancing toward the model, he felt uneasy about the receiver, Groth.

"I'm just a regular guy, actually. I don't mind a bit of company."

Her smile was wide and open, giving her a rustic look beneath her wet red curls.

"Were you getting out just now?"

"Yeah."

"Mind if I rinse in your house? That awful little man is snooping around in ours."

Hawkins felt vulnerable, not quite in control, but what could he say?

"Sure, no problem."

As they waded up, he mentioned his encounter with her husband.

"Max? What did you think of him?"

"Well, we only talked for a minute. Nice to meet you and such."

"Yes, Max is complicated. Takes a while to get to know, not to mention understand."

Hawkins opened the cottage and directed her to the shower, inviting her to use his robe afterward. To avoid any questions of propriety, he told her he'd be outside, having a look at the prefab work.

"Thank you," she said, smiling with her eyes as she held the bathroom door.

Hawkins grabbed a tee-shirt and got out of the cottage.

The crew was finishing up, one of them already walking down the beach toward the common area and dock. Hawkins suspected they'd been dawdling to watch Susanna cavort in the water. He waited while the others left and then sidled toward Fong's new home. It wasn't much, he found, not much better than the office shack one might find at a construction site. Maybe that was the idea, to get further use from it when more houses were built here. It fit with the apparent shrewdness of this receiver. There were no copper pipe fittings, Hawkins noticed. Prices must still be up.

When he guessed Susanna must have finished her shower, Hawkins drifted back toward his cottage. He reached the patio in back and took a few tentative steps to the back door. He peeked in its window. There was movement—Susanna, of course—coming into focus as his squinting eyes adjusted. With arms raised high, she was carrying the two parts of her wet bathing suit around the cottage, perhaps seeking a good place to dry them. She was nude.

Hawkins slipped away as quietly as he could.

Across the cove, in the living room of the model, Groth stood at the phone while Max puffed his pipe on the couch.

"Well, do you actually know anything about the body? Why do they want to hold you, then? Missing *what*? Organs—like out of the body? For Chrissakes Uh-huh, family in Australia, consulate, better investigation. Their tourist business, right. Well, I'm not forking out any bail money, Fong. You know we'll never see it again from these characters. I'm the receiver here. I can't let a bunch of pina coladas put the squeeze on me "

He was soon off the phone, leaving Fong unaided in his predicament.

"Damn " he exclaimed as he returned to his end of the couch.

"I take it," Max ventured, "Mr. Fong will not be returning on time."

"Damn, damn, *damn* " Groth answered. "Now I'm stuck in this crappy place because some tropical bozos don't know their asses from holes in the ground!"

Max decided to let him stew awhile, considered taking a walk. But a few more shouts and violent gestures seemed to lift Groth from his fury, at least temporarily, so he was free to return to their earlier discussion. He even took out his pipe.

"Anyway," he said, "getting back to your, uh, idea. We have a contract in place, right? You got in under the wire with Gaville. But the changes you're talking about would add hugely to the cost of construction. I can't have a lot more cash flowing out to the contractors. I already have to sweat their overruns. I can't free-wheel like Gaville did. As receiver I have to plug the dike, take no risks. I have to be Scrooge."

"Couldn't I just deal with the contractors myself? On the additions, I mean. I could negotiate, watch overruns, et cetera, myself."

"Sure you could, post-construction. After I have Gaville out of the picture."

"But that would be much more expensive. How about a rider on our contract in which I shoulder the additional cost?"

Groth shook his head, sage now amidst his pipe smoke.

"No can do. The costs would be impossible to keep separate, plus I'd be setting Gaville up for liability in case you defaulted. The judge would nail me to the wall."

Max frowned.

"I can provide ample financial references, if that's the problem."

"Actually, it's not just financial. This development, Cove of Dreams, is supposed to have a certain character. Something like, I don't know, peaceful seclusion for retirees or people getting away from it all. It was clear in their pitch, this location, the set-up of the place. What you're talking about—labs, equipment, a pro office—is at odds with all that. The additions would encroach on the planned space between the properties. You might see fit to bring in employees, and what about additional waste? See what I mean? It wouldn't be the Cove of Dreams any more, except in name only. The name would become a mockery."

Max took a puff himself, studying the owlish man beside him.

"You don't seem to have many dreamers coming, anyway."

Groth gave a grim smile.

"This place isn't my work. I just can't have more screw-ups on my watch."

They both puffed in silence.

"Look," Groth continued. "You want my advice? Given the incompetence at Gaville, I'm not sure this development is legally sound and met ethical standards. If you wanted out of your contract, there's probably some wiggle room."

Max took a moment before responding.

"No, I don't want to wiggle, Albert. Construction may proceed, and as soon as possible. The existing contract, if that's the best—"

The phone rang again. Groth jumped to answer it, as if welcoming the interruption.

"No " he was soon shouting. "Absolutely not I expect a swift hearing or questioning or whatever so he can get back to work. And think on this, friend: any bad press about holding foreigners and your tourist business takes a hit Lots of money lost for your country and who's gonna answer for *that*? You, right? Think about it. Now I want that man released and I'm not gonna pay any phony bail to you or anyone else "

The conversation proceeded while Max reflected on the couch. Across the cove, Hawkins sat in the shade of the prefab awaiting Susanna's exit from his cottage. He didn't know what she was up to, and he had no inclination to find out. At this age, this stage of life for him, when he'd finally resolved his penchant for isolation, someone like Susanna was a threat, elicited panic. It was foolish, he knew, from an objective standpoint, but then *he* was foolish, always had been, and unavoidably so. But he'd accepted his nature and even balanced it here with his visits to Lydia. He was at peace, didn't need anything more. And yet, it suddenly occurred to him, while he had no use for the "more" represented by Susanna, there was no denying the enchantment surrounding his meetings with Traci.

Susanna emerged from the cottage, dispelling his thoughts. She was wearing his royal blue robe. Her swimsuit dangled from one hand, apparently still wet. She sauntered toward him, not so much coy now as something else, perhaps insouciant. Was she miffed?

"Sorry I took so long."

"Hey, no problem."

"No problem? Really?"

Hawkins felt a welling irritation. He kept silent.

"Okay if I wear your robe home?"

She held up the damp swimsuit for inspection.

"Sure, go ahead."

It sounded wrong to him, as if he were ordering her to leave. But he'd been civil, hadn't he? Considerate. What more could be expected of him?

She started to smile but suddenly turned and walked off.

"See you," was all she said.

Hawkins watched for a moment, then headed for his cottage. He, too, needed a shower, the salty sea having dried on his body. He felt the dry oozing of the fine sand at his feet, somehow lacking its usual degree of comfort, its impersonal intimacy. He found that Susanna had left the door of the cottage ajar with the air conditioner running. She'd also had a snack, an empty yogurt container and spoon lying on his table amidst a galaxy of toast crumbs. There was also a wine bottle, empty now but half-full of Cabernet when last he'd seen it.

Hawkins turned off the air-con to save the solar cells. Returning to the door, he watched Susanna on the other side of the cove, still walking in his robe. I am what I am, he thought. No more, no less. You might not like that but nothing's going to change it.

But again the image of Traci flitted in his memory.

15.

A tricycle stopped before one of the government buildings in the center of the capital. Lydia alighted, paid the driver, and greeted guards to whom she was a familiar sight. She wore a shiny rose-colored dress today, her hair tied back loosely with a matching velvet band. She removed her hat as she entered the building, having worn one, as usual, against the sun rather than for fashion. She ascended a wide stone staircase, worn toward the center from generations of use. She passed a few office staff, her nominal coworkers, on her way to Mr. Ub's office at the end of the hall. It was unusual for him to call her in, disregarding her appointments, but they both knew her loyalty made that a non-issue. She opened his door and entered.

Mr. Ub wore expensive suits in the office, as he did at social and government events, but without his cummerbund and medals. Such items, he'd confided to Lydia, did not impress foreign business people, and perhaps even marked him as antiquated. He sat now behind his expansive desk, accompanied by a young police captain who turned in his chair as Lydia entered. Lydia recognized him.

"We're just finishing," Mr. Ub informed her. Then, to the captain, "You've met Miss Coe, my special assistant?"

"I think so, yes, at a function or two."

"You recall Captain Rua?" asked Mr. Ub.

Lydia murmured her assent, exchanging polite smiles. Her strongest memory of the captain, however, was of his wildly dancing with a woman who looked like a prostitute. He'd been out of uniform and more or less drunk. It was in a club Lydia visited incognito, her hair in a dowdy arrangement and her face behind garish dark glasses. She occasionally went out this way to spy on the world, to see what was going on without having to play her role, to relax. At this particular club there were often quality people—lawyers from the justice ministry, medical people, professors. This was an off night, however, made more so by the arrival of Captain Rua and his group. As his grotesque performance ended, he noticed Lydia watching from the bar. Struck by her look of tacky aging, he turned away with a sneer and went to join his friends.

"You look most beautiful today," he said now.

Lydia murmured thanks, reminded again of the shallowness of sunny smiles.

Once he'd gone, shutting the door behind him, Lydia sat before the desk. Mr. Ub settled into his gravest mien.

"There is clearly a problem," he said. "Complicated. Threatening."

He hesitated, his lips pressed together, his gaze past her shoulder.

"Can I help?" Lydia ventured.

"Unfortunately, not much. You've been quite valuable, but this involves the darker side of things. We're on the defensive, it seems."

He looked at her directly.

"I'd like to think it was just incompetence, bad as that is. Then it might be fixed and explained somehow, smoothed over. But this release of a body—Tabor, from Project Island—with parts missing inside, questions about the death, nobody knowing what happened—it smacks of something else. Captain Rua is in charge of the investigation. He led the recovery detail that brought the body in. They've detained the man who called them, who found the body, a caretaker out there. He's clearly not at fault, has no more information, but they're holding him to show we're doing something. It can't go on, of course. We'll need a real solution. Our commercial standing is quite fragile in the world. We can't afford international scandal."

Was she here, Lydia wondered, to commiserate? Was it simply her presence, her listening, that Mr. Ub had summoned her for?

"You said there wasn't much I could do about it. Was there something small, then? Any way I can help, you know I'm ready to act."

Mr. Ub smiled, seeming for a moment his usual solid self.

"Of course I know that. But this is beyond your purview, Lydia. I don't need you to act, actually, but to refrain from what you've been doing."

Lydia froze, dreading his knowledge of the secret that would ruin her.

"Sir?"

"I know your work on the B List has meant much to you, as it has to me also, of course. The ministry is most appreciative, as is the palace. But this situation with Tabor suggests a possible misuse of influence, a need to tighten the reins. I don't like to think a Best Citizen might abuse the pin's influence, but I'm afraid we have to consider it, protect against it in the future. As of today, recruitment for the B List is suspended indefinitely, as are the meetings and activities of the members."

Lydia relaxed a little, unsure what to say. She settled for a look of disappointment.

"I've spoken with a colleague in the culture ministry," Mr. Ub continued. "The palace has been wanting to expand our music programs, send students abroad to compete. There's a desire to have a national orchestra some day. With your teaching background, we think you'd do well in coordinating the program, bringing together the students, teachers, and parents to raise the standards. Later will come the international arrangements, the good will and attention to detail that you're so good with. I'm sure you'll be fine in the position, Lydia. You should do well. Your salary will continue on the same level."

Lydia relaxed some more, allowed her downcast look to melt to tears.

"I'll miss working with you, Mr. Ub."

"I'll miss it also, Lydia, but I'm sure we'll be seeing each other sometimes. And before I forget, I must ask you to contact me if you hear anything helpful on Tabor. You may bypass Captain Rua. I have little confidence in his handling this. He only has his commission, not to mention his rank, because his father is a senator. Otherwise he'd be working in the casino. You also need not report on what your friend Mr. Hawkins says. He and I have a separate understanding. He seems like a fine man."

He smiled fondly with his appraisal of Hawkins, eyes lingering on Lydia's.

"Yes," she replied, "he is."

Leaving the building later, Lydia was disconcerted. She'd grown used to her work routine, made it part of her identity, and now it was gone. She turned to take a farewell look at the entrance. One of the guards, misunderstanding, stepped forward and hailed a loafing tricycle driver down the street. And thus she was hustled on her way.

Lydia was driven out of the city center and through the commercial ring, skirting the waterfront. She passed the turn for Neptune's Pride, where she was wont to meet Hawkins, and continued toward the city's tattered edges. Near the turn for the airport was another cluster of businesses. She had the driver stop before a clothing store, waited as he drove off, then walked a short way to the Bad Gong restaurant.

It was gloomy inside despite the curtains being open. An elderly couple sat by the window in front, having tea. The only other customer was a big man near the back, eating from several plates with beer bottles next to them. A wraith-like waiter moved in the shadows. Lydia allowed her eyes to adjust, then approached the big man as he watched her.

"I got hungry waiting," said Hans. "What did he want?"

Lydia hesitated as the waiter drifted near.

"Just tea," she told him.

She then related to Hans her conversation with Mr. Ub. She spoke calmly until describing the change in her job, unable to control her sense of loss. Her voice wavered and trailed off, but Hans didn't seem to notice, having his own priorities.

"So there's no specific person they suspect?" he asked. "Our man and whoever helped him are as safe as anyone else?"

"Yes."

"What about money? Do you think he'll want more?"

"I don't think so. He'd be in danger himself if he talked."

"Yes, well, just in case—"

He slid an envelope across the table to her.

"I don't think this will be necessary."

"Well, you'll be ready if it is."

Hans called the waiter to clear his dishes, ordered another beer.

"Dr. Kassander appreciates your help," he told Lydia. "I believe he mentioned a work visa for you, Europe or America.

If things are getting awkward here for you, perhaps we should move ahead on that."

Lydia sat up, tried to focus on the proposal, the reality of such a great move.

"Well, what do you say? It would be good for all of us. You'd be safe from investigation and they'd have no link to the project."

"Yes, it's something I want. It just seems so sudden."

"It will always seem sudden. Every great change seems sudden. And drastic, perhaps. But that's what makes it great, its effect. That's why you should want it to happen."

While they conversed in the Bad Gong, Mr. Ub stood at a window of his office in the ministry. His gaze took in he street below, the stone buildings, a bit of sea, the endless sky with its haze of heat. He missed the old life, he realized, the years before technology and economics made the world smaller. He saw himself as a boy, playing with others of his class in the dusty byways, the fragrant gardens. The older generations looked on with hope, relieved that the ravages of war had passed them by. Now he and his country had come to this, shrinking roles that were nonetheless vulnerable to foreign or domestic sabotage. A single incident could spotlight their insignificance, expose their culture as anachronism. With an even worse economy, disaffection of youth, the Kingdom would be a humiliated vassal state. He and his colleagues could do little to stop it.

A bird crossed his view, winging up over the buildings. Mr. Ub watched it pass from sight, then saw instead his condo in California, an overseas investment that was now something more. Yes, he thought, I can live among men like Hawkins, men of business who needn't fear humiliation. Men whose visions are free from unreality. Beacons of rational thought.

16.

    Susanna stood in the doorway of the model, looking out at Groth floating on his back in the cove. She felt rising disdain as he rippled the water with his arms. Behind her the door of the microwave stood open, the remains of an exploded fish steak inside, courtesy of Groth. It was the second time this week. The other time she'd had an incinerated calzone to remove before she could have her lunch.

    There were many irritations from the man. It wasn't herself, she thought, because she lived with a man she accepted and loved in her way. But Max was neat and clean, even stylish, and considerate almost to a fault, whereas Groth was an obnoxious pig. Besides the kitchen, he always left the bathroom a mess, soiling all the towels and using much of her shampoo. Once she'd returned from birdwatching to find her underwear rifled.

    "Try to ignore him," Max advised. "He'll be gone any day now."

    But the caretaker was still in jail so Groth was staying longer. Anyway, how was she supposed to ignore him, these things he did? That might even have been him the other night, rustling around the half-bath window while she was in there—a peeping Tom! And then he had the gall to try to badger Max through her, push him into cancelling their construction. That had been another time when Max wasn't around.

"You don't seem happy here," Groth said with fake sympathy.

She gave him what must have been an ugly look.

"I mean," he went on, "you've hardly arrived and it seems you're ready to leave."

She gave a half-shrug, looked back at her magazine.

"It was Max's idea. A retreat for when he needs it." I just go along, she thought to herself, but wouldn't say it to Groth.

"Guess it's kind of rough for you," he persisted nonetheless, "an isolated place you don't really want to be."

She crisply turned a couple of pages.

"I'm fine."

"You can easily get out of the contract, you know. I have full authority to approve."

"Talk to Max!"

"What's that magazine you're reading?" he asked after a pause.

"A catalog," she almost snarled. "Copper pipe fittings."

Susanna wondered now if she should confront him about the microwave. However burdensome, it wasn't close to being the most serious of his offenses. She didn't want him to think the bathroom peeping and underwear fetish were no big thing for her, maybe even turned her on. She'd better hold her fire, she thought, perhaps complain to someone else.

She turned away from the floater in the cove and prepared to make a salad.

17.

The door to Popeye's cage in the EAU stood wide open. Most of the animals were indifferent to this anomaly, but Poobah stared with consternation at the building's exit, its door not fully closed. It was evening, as it had been for Popeye's other forays. Poobah had seen him discover the means of escape, then venture outside for increasing periods, always to hurry back. Tonight, however, he'd been out an uncomfortably long time. Poobah was growing restless, envy stirring in him as his comrade's freedom grew.

Outside, Popeye ambled to the edge of the compound and toward the southern shore. He kept glancing back at first but, catching a familiar scent, scuttled eagerly toward a growth of small trees and shrubs. It gave way to a descending litter of boulders that eventually dotted the sea, but Popeye stopped short in the bushes. There was another scent now, and another voice talking with the small human who was kind to him.

"So I was just drifting," Hawkins said, "though I guess I looked different to others. Purposeful and such."

"But wasn't there one you cared about most?" Traci asked. "One you couldn't forget even if you wanted to?"

"I just remember fragments of relationships. Together they might make a whole, but—no, no. There was never the advanced stage, or stages. Where a relationship dominates your life."

"Not that it's good, necessarily. That dominating love."

"No. Maybe that's what I was afraid of. Getting cut off from the rest of life, missing out on things."

"Missing out, yes. I suppose there can be so much to life."

"And so little time, as they say."

"So the problem, you think, may be in life itself, that it's too short?"

"Well, yeah. For some people, anyway. Of course, there's quality of life, too. Time moves pretty slow when it's not there."

"But if you have the quality, or it's available to you, then the issue becomes to live longer. Doesn't it? Perhaps as long as you can?"

"Well, sure," Hawkins chuckled. "Sky's the limit."

Sensing that his friend wasn't in danger, but also was not available, Popeye slunk back from the scene. Behind the cover of brush, he ambled westward toward taller trees on the far reach of Essquibo's property. He eventually came to the chain-link fence with the Cove of Dreams beyond. He surveyed the moonlit expanse of land, the gentle sweep of water it enclosed. He noted the two small buildings, the prefab and Hawkins's cottage, both dark. The prefab stirred a memory of his cage and he glanced backward, momentarily anxious. But he was energized by discovery so curiosity prevailed, especially when he saw lights to the northwest, the model standing on the far point. Staying to the clear strip by the fence, Popeye continued his exploration.

Coming from the opposite direction, puffing casually on his pipe, Max reflected as he walked past the properties. The emptiness here, the delays in development, the incompetence, would eventually grate on Susanna. Remoteness, seclusion, even for a little while and with pressing purpose, weren't for everyone. He couldn't expect her to be patient and appreciate its value. It was, after all, her unlikeness to him that he'd found attractive, that was her value. For him and for society she provided a forceful balance to his intensely ascetic, fanatically private nature. She liked the security he offered, the modest celebrity, but her need to leave would accelerate and he would have to accompany her. Her flirting tendency was an outlet for her, might have helped keep them here, but the lack of prospects only frustrated her. She found Groth repulsive and the hermit was some kind of crazy virgin. Max had been amused at first when she'd appeared in Hawkins's robe, but Susanna soon put him right.

He approached the prefab, Fong's imminent arrival coming to mind. Perhaps, he thought, a more promising target for her. But what's that—up by the fence?

A bulky form was moving through shadows of trees on the Essquibo side.

Must be one of the guards, Max thought. Looks like he's drunk. Well, Hans mentioned they'd economized in hiring them. You get what you pay for.

Earlier in the day, Max had been Hans's guest in the lunchroom of the project. Hans had expressed belief in the use of nanotechnology to prevent entropy in the regeneration of human cells. The tiny robots or organisms infused into the subject might be self-replicating, but would in any case be subject to wireless control from without. Current financial limits kept the project from developing this strategy, Hans confided, but Max's involvement might speed things up. Max found it mildly interesting, said he'd think about it. Before he left, Hans led him to a corner of the reception area and talked of something else, ideas of Dr. Kassander. Either to supplement a brain transplant, or to program the new brain of a clone, Max might assist with mind transfer, the scanning and mapping of a subject's brain to produce complete files of his thought processes, memories, et cetera. Max had nodded thoughtfully, seeing the promise in this immediate application of radical new software. Success would be quite lucrative.

And our fame would skyrocket, he thought now as he walked. Susanna would be pleased, bubbly with joy. She could throw parties, flirt with big shots, stand in for me on talk shows. Perhaps if I float it by her, she won't mind hanging tough on the island for a while, or returning when Essquibo is ready for me.

He came to the end of the fence near the southern shore, noticed that Hawkins's cottage was dark.

Guess our hermit goes to bed early, Max thought. Damn him for his purity Or is it purism here? People have no idea how their idiotic ideals can get in the way, the damage they can do. What an idiot

He rounded the edge of the fence and found increasingly rocky, uneven footing as he traversed the southern shore. He had to pick his way carefully, his gaze downward except when he paused to view the sea, indigo under the moon. He felt a comforting solitude as his gaze pierced endlessly into infinity. Moving on, he noticed the sea intruding between the outermost boulders, forming a tiny archipelago. He moved inward, toward the rough growth overhead, but soon realized he was not alone. Two voices, male and female, carried to where he crouched near the brush, then ducked into it. He was loath to interrupt a tryst. From his vantage point he was shocked to recognize Hawkins, the supposedly purist hermit. Wondering what sort of woman had managed to entice him, Max strained awkwardly for a better view. He almost dropped his pipe as he caught sight of Traci, her face and hands luminous under the moon, her loose white garment drab by comparison, her rich fall of long black hair, the flash from her eyes.

"I shouldn't have told you so much," she said.

"You can trust me," Hawkins replied.

"But can you handle it, the knowledge? Most people aren't ready for it. Not till there's clear, concrete proof. Irrefutable. But I wanted you to see—you know, that you have options."

"I appreciate that. I don't think I can use them, but I appreciate your telling me. And I appreciate *you*."

A hesitation.

"I don't see what can come of this," said Traci. "I mean, I'm not clear."

"Neither am I, but—"

Hawkins seemed at a loss.

"Maybe," Traci ventured, "we can just share our uncertainty, go down a foggy path together, like children in a strange garden."

Hawkins laughed uncertainly.

"Except we're not children," he said. "Especially me."

"But maybe something like it, if you want. The extra life ahead, unending even, and a *better* life—"

Her voice trailed off in a tone of entreaty.

"For *us*?" Hawkins finished.

Traci answered by raising her hands, holding his face when he came forward. They kissed, a profound statement of unity in the moonlight.

Unnerved, Max backed into the brush. Above the rocky shore, he moved westward toward taller trees and the boundary fence. What in the world, he wondered, was going on there? Like a goddess she was—glowing in a lab coat—offering eternal life to that nutcase. Max recalled his talk with Hans, considered the secrecy of this place, its shadowy backers. He didn't have the full story on this work, but he sensed it was big and he well might want in.

He worked his way around the edge of the fence, back into the Cove of Dreams development. Still excited, he relit his pipe and puffed with vigor as he strode northward close to the fence. There was a rustling of brush as someone approached clumsily on the other side. That guard again, Max thought. The thick form slowed as it passed him, indistinct in the shadows of trees.

"Good evening " Max declared crisply.

The only reply was a robust snort.

"Good Lord," Max muttered, "what an animal "

He quickened his pace as Popeye continued to his cage.

18.

Sweating profusely, Groth marched through the city center with Fong at his side. It had taken some time to secure the release, and Groth was angered by the byzantine procedures. Having not received payment, the authorities had insisted Groth pick the prisoner up, taking full responsibility. The receiver had to complete many forms and they even took his picture. It was finally behind him but irritation lingered, leaving Groth disinclined to commiserate with Fong on his experience. He also had other business here, wanting to make the most of the trip.

"Maybe we should take the tricycle," Fong suggested. "It's very far to the water taxi."

"We're not going back yet," Groth replied. "I have to see a deputy minister."

"Do you have an appointment?"

Groth frowned at his companion as if he'd said something senseless.

They arrived at the building and breezed past the outer guards, though one turned to watch until a guard met the visitors inside. They were patted down and allowed to proceed. They soon found Mr. Ub's outer office, a surprised assistant trying to handle Groth's intrusion. Overmatched, the assistant checked with his boss and waved the visitors forward, but Groth raised an arm before Fong.

"Confidential," he stated glibly.

Fong took a seat next to a potted palm.

Within his office, Ub was expansive, welcoming Groth and even offering a cigar.

"Thanks, I have a pipe."

"Feel free to light."

Ub lit up himself, so Groth brought out his pipe and added his smoke to the billows. Though soaked with sweat and not relishing heat, he wouldn't allow Ub to seem more relaxed.

"So," said Mr. Ub, "have you progressed with your work here?"

"Yes," Groth answered, "I'd say I have. But I'm not finished yet."

He hesitated but Ub was impassive, nodding slightly behind his desk.

"So you have more to do?"

"I might. I *very well* might. Oh, I've stopped the bleeding, financially I mean, but there's the question how Gaville got into this. This financial *mess*."

"Ah. But surely that's very complicated. They have many other holdings, correct?"

"Yes, and they're being dealt with. But this was by far their shakiest venture, the *coup de grâce* to their financial functioning."

"Sounds rather melodramatic," Ub smiled.

"It's a serious matter " Groth retorted, then caught himself. He had to be smooth on this.

"The thing is," he continued, "I'm not convinced the original purchase of the island, the joint purchase by Gaville and Essquibo, was entirely valid. In fact, it's highly flawed."

Mr. Ub held his cigar before his face, raised his eyes as if considering.

"What do you mean?" he finally asked.

"Well, there was no real title search. The only history was conveyance to you by another government entity, the official essentially a colleague. And I understand there's this fraternity between you, the 'B List,' creating even more of a conflict."

"The Best Citizens List has been dissolved."

"Well, it wasn't at the time of the sale. And anyway there's more. The purchase resulted in tenancy in common, immediately followed by an order of partition. The tenancy in common didn't last a single day, so it's questionable whether it legally existed at all. And if it didn't exist, then neither did the sale."

Mr. Ub shifted in his chair.

"Mr. Groth, a judge of the Kingdom was present to sign the order of partition."

"Fine, but did it *mean* anything? Were they the *legal owners* yet?"

"It seems you're grabbing at straws."

"Yeah? Well, try this one. What about the lenders for Gaville and Essquibo? You went ahead with partitioning without advising them, getting their okay."

"Essquibo was fully financed by their investors. Their attorney had full authority."

"Yeah? Well, that wasn't the case with Gaville. And now they're gonna take a bath "

I could use one myself, Groth thought. He had to restrain himself, stop sweating.

"Gaville got the smaller share of island," he continued. "For sure the lenders would've wanted a say on that. You shrunk their collateral."

"The agreement was between the co-tenants, the purchasers if you will."

Groth sat back, puffed his pipe, he and Ub eyeing each other through swirls of smoke.

"I assure you," Ub smiled, "the sale was entirely valid under our laws."

"The document signed by the prince," Groth ventured, affecting coolness.

"The order of autonomy for Project Island."

"Yes. I noticed it was dated the day before the sale."

"So?" Mr. Ub frowned. "All the documents were prepared in advance. A signature from the palace requires an appointment, so we got it the day before."

"Still," Groth insisted with half-closed eyes, "the island was then autonomous before the sale. So the mainland did not have legal authority to sell it."

Ub laughed at this.

"Oh come now, Mr. Groth. It was clearly a matter of necessity under our laws and customs, which are the deciding authority here, you know. And who on the island could have exercised autonomy the day before? The sea birds? A marooned rodent or two?"

Groth felt the mockery, thought he may have gone too far. His old pushiness might be surfacing—the urge to show all he knew and get credit for it, as he once tried to please his teachers. But he had one more card to play, albeit a weak one, and he couldn't stop babbling.

"Then there's the fishing rights issue," he said.

"Fishing rights?"

"They're being disputed in waters closer to Project Island than to either of the countries claiming them."

"Well, what about it?"

"It should have been disclosed before the sale as a defect in the property."

Mr. Ub gave Groth a probing look, as if verifying he'd heard correctly, then yielded to a deeper laughter than before. He puffed on his cigar, laughing a little more as he drew it away.

"Commercial fishing at the Cove of Dreams Is one of your retirees going to bring a fishing boat in, have the crew live with him? Would his neighbors enjoy the stink?"

"These are all solid points I've made," Groth insisted. "I'd appreciate your cooperation in having the sale nullified and reversing the inappropriate transfer of funds."

He stopped talking, determined not to not water down his position further. Pinned by his owlish glare, Mr. Ub sobered but, laying aside his cigar, assumed a sympathetic mien.

"Mr. Groth, with all respect, we both know that is not going to happen. The transaction was entirely proper within the laws and regulations of our Kingdom, which are the only standards that apply here. In addition, there has been considerable building and other changes on the island, so it's no longer the commodity that was sold. You cannot exchange a pair of shoes after you wear a hole in them. I know you have a job to do here, and I respect that. I understand you had to give this a try. But it seems you've exhausted your points and I feel no compunction in, well, setting them aside."

Groth was silent, seeing the game was over. He rose as if to leave, but Ub raised a hand.

"There may be another way," he said. "A way I can help you."

Groth settled back as Ub touched the intercom on his desk.

"Hold any calls and don't disturb us for a while."

Ub then got up himself.

"Excuse me a moment. I'll just stretch my legs."

He slowly strode to the window, viewed the city outside, then returned and, to Groth's puzzlement, unplugged his intercom. Instead of returning to his chair, Ub came to the front of his desk and sat on its edge close to Groth, speaking in a hushed tone.

"Now," he said, "perhaps we can help *each other*, sir."

"I'm listening," Groth replied gamely.

He tried to show no emotion as the proposition unfolded. It was an offer to buy Gaville's portion of Project Island as a new transaction, but with an odd stipulation. Somehow or other, Mr. Ub was also to receive a worthwhile interest in the island project of Essquibo Institute. Negotiation with the project was to be done by Groth, with closing of the Cove sale dependent on his success. Mr. Ub would remain in the background.

"You'll have your profits from the sale to influence them, and I'll give them a piece or two of the Cove as well."

Groth was inwardly flustered by the plan, an anomaly in his way of doing things. He was a standard-procedures man who feared the least challenge on ethics. But this was a different place, much different, with its own ersatz rules, and he was desperate to untangle the Cove of Dreams and Gaville Associates. He couldn't just leave things a mess and slink into retirement, exiting on a profoundly sour note. He was Albert Groth, after all, with his reputation as highly competent, his identity as an accomplished man, and these must be perpetuated.

"Let's talk some figures," he said.

In the outer office, sitting by the potted palm, Fong was talking on his cell phone with his son. He'd wanted Zing to know he was free, that his steady employer had come through, that Zing should now focus on stabilizing his own situation. But the son's opportunism asserted itself, presenting Fong again with a painful contrast between Zing and himself.

"No, no, what are you talking about, sue everyone? They would just throw me out of here, deport me. I couldn't get to my job, it would be gone. Sue *who*? The company? About the bail, the delay, I see. Well, I don't know it was their responsibility. And again, the job would be gone. You have to be careful, Zing. You don't throw away something steady just to try a quick grab. Things don't work that way."

On the other side of the palm plant and a little down the hall, Captain Rua stood listening with an eavesdropping device. He was pointing a small wand toward the plant, a wire leading from the wand to an earphone he wore. He'd heard nothing suspicious, confirming the conclusion that Fong had nothing to do with Tabor's death or mishandling of the body. Rua continued to listen, however, since he had no other leads and it made him feel professional. It also occurred to him that Zing sounded rather sleazy, that an Interpol check might be justified. Even if it turned up nothing, thought Rua, the check would enhance his investigation, give it some class.

The door to Mr. Ub's office opened. Groth came out striding purposefully, chin raised and holding his pipe. Rua put away his device.

"Let's go," said Groth to Fong, barely breaking stride.

He breezed past Rua, paying him no notice, but Fong gave a nervous nod. Rua answered with about half his usual smile. He followed them until they disappeared down the stairs, soon to be trailed by a man outside. They'd be returning to the island, Rua saw, so he could turn his thoughts again to the sports car he desired.

19.

Hans stood at the boundary fence, viewing the remains of sunset through metal webbing. This was where Max had encountered a drunken guard, he said, though that was in full night and with any moonlight blocked by overhanging trees. Not enough to confront someone on, Hans thought. Too bad. He'd wanted from the beginning to have a better-trained unit, but there was that irritating parsimony when the project was launched. It might become possible—should, actually—as the value of what was being guarded became obvious.

Viewing the fiery sky beyond the undeveloped Cove of Dreams, Hans reflected on how he'd been doing well in his home country, how his coming here had been questionable. He was living comfortably, with a solid and developing career before him. The Essquibo project appeared quite speculative. But, as an employee, he had no proprietary rights to his work, no matter how significant, and he was living in a socialist state. The offer to join the project presented a chance to rise above his highest possible level back home.

"Once in a lifetime," he commented aloud.

There were bumps in the road, of course. Financing to date hadn't been focused on strategies he would have preferred, ones that drew more on his talents and experience. But he had confidence in Kassander's precision and skill, and in Traci's knowledge and commitment, so he expected to share in great success. In the meantime he'd apply himself assiduously to his duties as assigned, including this involvement with security.

Turning from the fence, he started back the way he'd come, toward the dock and path to the compound. Seeing the play of reddish light among the trees, however, he decided to take a shortcut. He was just emerging on the other side when he noticed two figures in the distance, standing close and conversing. One of the guards and a woman in lab coat.

"Off-duty, I hope," Hans muttered.

He watched from the shadows as the guard raised a hand to the woman's shoulder. She didn't respond physically though she was speaking to him. The guard removed his hand and looked down, the woman continuing to speak. Feeling suddenly foolish, Hans turned from the scene and crossed diagonally away from the couple.

He would definitely have to pursue that replacement of the guard unit, Hans resolved. He'd revisit it with Kassander as soon as possible, stress that the need must be understood by Essquibo. Kassander himself could appreciate loose ends, loose cannons.

20.

"Poobah was bad today," Ana informed Traci.

She'd just entered the synthesis lab, dust showing on her smock and in her hair.

"What happened?"

"He started throwing dirt at Popeye, scooping up big handfuls. He wouldn't stop and Jun couldn't restrain him. He had to call Mulo and they were wrestling with him. I stayed with Popeye and got dirty too."

Jun and Mulo were two of the guards, Jun usually escorting Ana during the chimps' exercise sessions.

"Are you all right?" Traci asked.

"Oh, yes. Just dirty. I don't know what's got into him lately. They used to get along just fine. Even after the transplants, at first."

"Well, Popeye's been sort of—I don't know—aloof lately. He won't eat till you leave, just leaves the treat pellets. It started before he got the chromosome, but maybe it's become nuanced in some way, a difference we don't see but Poobah picks up on, resents."

"Are his metabolic figures still okay?"

"Yes, and so are Chico's."

Chico was the smaller of the two new males. As a control, he too had been infused with the new chromosome received by Popeye.

"So, except for Poobah, we're agreed on the success."

Traci hesitated, fingering the edge of Cyril's notes, thinking of Hawkins.

"We need to observe," she said. "The objective is human recipients, mostly transplant patients, and solid marketing potential. We have to be sure, as sure as we can be."

Elsewhere in the compound, Lydia sat with Dr. Kassander in his office. The doctor was edgy, as always when taken from his work, and he had Albert Groth waiting to see him next. But for now it was enough to deal with this lovely woman, to be gentle in having to dispose of her. The project was an overriding priority that had to be painstakingly protected. In another place, at another time, he would have enjoyed continuing to see Lydia. But here and now, with a budding investigation by petty officials, he wanted her out of their reach, which unfortunately meant out of his.

"You won't reconsider on Europe? Particularly in Hans's country, you could have a much better arrangement."

"No," Lydia answered, "I've thought it through."

"Very well. Hans will be at the Bad Gong with everything you need, and he'll accompany you to your flight. You're prepared to travel light?"

Lydia couldn't help reflecting. She'd be abandoning most of her wardrobe, perhaps a

large part of her identity. Today she wore a sleeveless peach-colored dress for the last time. But she had to sacrifice to avoid arousing suspicion.

"Yes, and my papers are all in order. I'm ready to go."

Kassander regarded her.

"You're leaving the place that was your home for so long, the people you know. Who knows when you can return? Vancouver is a cold city, though there are worse there. It might be difficult to move south, over the border. You might have to marry an American. I can make no further promises after this relocation. You are sure you accept this?"

"Yes."

Kassander allowed a rare smile.

"Then we are finished. I don't know if we'll talk again. The work here will take most of my time and energy for a long time. But I wish you well, Lydia, and thank you for your help."

"Thank *you*, sir. Good-bye."

As she passed through the reception area, Lydia noticed a pudgy man with glasses scowling at her. One of the guards stood nearby, dividing his attention between Groth and the entrance to the compound outside. Security was spread thin today, Lydia thought. The guard noticed her and murmured something to Groth, who aggressively snatched up his briefcase and stomped toward Dr. Kassander's office.

Outside, Lydia descended the wide path into the common area. It was a pleasant day on the island, the sun warming her shoulders with a soft caress, the sea breeze gentler than she'd expected. She attended to the sound of her steps as she crossed the landing area, her heels on the wood. The tropic buzz was her only accompaniment. How strange it seemed at this moment that she could be at the center of some sort of intrigue. She was innocent, of course, of any evil intent. She'd done as she'd always done to make a life for herself, get by in this backwater of the world. This time it meant taking flight, but it was clearly a necessary step, something she'd have done in her youth if she'd known better and had the means.

She continued down the path on the other side, into the Cove of Dreams.

What, she wondered, could she say to Hawkins? He wasn't just some business deal she was cutting loose. In a way, he was the inspiration for this, her big step. He'd given her perspective on life, a sense of possibilities beyond the Kingdom. We have limits in our natures and in time, but we can accept these limits and grow with what we have, reach the best possible state. He himself had made a radical change, moving here. She was doing the same in the opposite direction. She'd been refreshed by his attitude, she realized, even before this opportunity, this necessity, took form. It was at the core of her feeling for him.

She passed the northern point of the cove, the model off to her right, reached the beach and turned southward. She walked the path that fronted the properties, a ridge of firmer footing above the sand. She'd worn a smaller-brimmed hat today, anticipating more of a wind, so her view was unimpeded. Dr. Kassander, she realized, had of course been right. She would naturally feel some regret on leaving here. There were so many details that she was used to and were part of her—in her apartment, her work, her memories. She still had her sisters here, and old school friends, the friendly greetings of people who respected her. But then, too, as dusk closed in and shouts rose here and there, and on uneventful weekends, the Kingdom could seem such a small, stagnant, suffocating place. The tacky clubs, children playing in the dirt, tinny music on the street, the smells, the corruption, the archaic and useless customs, the absurd royalty. All of it unchanging, Lydia thought, at least during her lifetime. What good was it to be respected in a place that itself had no respect in the world?

She eventually passed the prefab, where Fong was working on the door. He quickly returned her wave and went back to his task. Thinking he might be out of sorts, Lydia continued on to Hawkins's cottage.

"Ah," he greeted her, "now my day can start."

His usual easy smile, pool cue lightly held in hand.

"Hey," he said, "what's the matter?"

She hadn't moved or spoken, the tear she'd shed her only expression.

"Nothing," she managed.

"The wind maybe," he said, "a little sand."

"Must be that."

He stood aside and closed the door when she'd entered.

"A little calimansi, then? Or maybe a beer?"

"The juice is fine."

They sat in the living room on his couch, leaving space between them as always when they met. A mild breeze passed through the screens as if they were outside.

"Mr. Fong was very busy," she commented. "Seemed he didn't want to be bothered."

"There was a break-in there. He's replacing the lock. He lives there now since they kicked him out of the model."

"Kicked him out?"

Hawkins explained about the Hoorts and Groth, who was staying longer than expected.

"How awful," Lydia responded. "And then the little hut they give him is damaged. I can see why he's not so happy."

"Actually," Hawkins grimaced, "that's not the worst of it."

"Oh?"

He hesitated.

"There was a big pile of feces he had to clear out. Sorry."

Lydia looked at him wide-eyed, set down her glass.

"God Who could have done something like that?"

"The people in the model think it was one of the guards from the project. Max, the husband there, says he saw one of them drunk around our area."

Lydia shook her head.

"Will you be all right?" she asked.

"Oh, sure. Whoever it was won't come around again. They went in Fong's place because it was empty. He was still tied up in the capital."

They recounted events leading to the investigation, eventually coming to Lydia's new role and the demise of the B List.

"Do I have to return my pin?" Hawkins smiled.

"Not that I've heard. You can keep it as a memento."

There was a catch in her throat as she said this, but Hawkins didn't seem to notice.

"I don't suppose they're issuing refunds," he continued.

She smiled coyly, as if reminding him this was the Kingdom.

"The official position is that it's suspended, not abolished."

"Ah, I see. Well, that about covers everything for them."

Lydia kept her eyes on her glass as she swirled calimansi juice. She had to get down to business, she knew.

"Mr. Ub happened to mention—"

She hesitated, not wanting to equivocate with Hawkins. But his eyes were waiting, trusting whatever she would say.

"He said you were, you know, reporting to him on what transpires here on the island."

Hawkins seemed mystified at first, then nodded in recollection, adjusting his sprawl on the couch.

"That was at the party, when we went to his house. I thought it was part of the B-List thing so I went along with it. And it was info on the project he wanted, not anything about *us*. But how would I know anything about the project? I never had anything to report."

Lydia waited a moment, drawing on her will.

"I wanted to ask you, well, if you could keep it that way."

He gave her a puzzled look, then chuckled.

"I don't see why not." A hesitation. "Is there something you want to tell me?"

She leaned toward him but stayed on her end of the couch.

"I just don't want you getting involved in whatever's going on. If it's something not so good, you might be hurt. Promise me you'll stay out of it, Merv. If you happen to discover something, don't report it to Mr. Ub. Please."

Hawkins again looked puzzled, deeply this time.

"Sure, but—"

She moved a bit toward him, close enough to take his hand.

"It's important to me," she said.

He smiled. She'd succeeded. She could move on, quickly while she still dared.

"Will you ever go back, do you think?"

"Back? You mean America?"

"Yes. Do you want to at all, deep down?"

"Well, I don't know. I sold everything to come here. Made a clean break. Maybe for a visit, I guess."

"But there must be things you miss, the day-to-day life you knew."

"There's things I'd miss *here*. There's you."

She smiled, almost kissed him. But she held herself back. She knew she should tell him everything, but also knew she couldn't. She could afford no risk.

"I only ask because, if I were to emigrate some day, I think it would be to where you came from. If you were also there, of course, it would be so much better."

Hawkins cogitated a bit.

"I don't know what to say. Maybe when I visit, if I do, we could go together and I could give you the grand tour. No harm in thinking about it."

"No," Lydia smiled, "no harm at all."

She kissed him quickly and pulled back.

"Want some more juice?" he asked.

"No, I have to meet the water taxi."

"Ah, this was a day trip."

"Yes. You know I wish it weren't, but these new duties of mine, the hours—"

"I understand. No problem, my dear."

He seemed to take it so easily, she thought. Was there even relief in his voice?

They kissed again briefly when she left the cottage, Hawkins watching as she set off down the path. Fong was nowhere in sight, but he'd picked up his tools and the new lock was securely fastened. It flashed in the sun as Lydia passed.

21.

The Ub mansion was locked and quiet, with minimal lighting, its customary state for the late hour. Mrs. Ub was asleep, resting for travel the next day, but her husband was in the library standing over drafts of letters he'd written. He held a drink and had already drunk more than he normally did. This would have to be his last, he thought, though he was still stirred by the anger he'd had to control while writing.

"He was very upset," his assistant had said, referring to Kassander's call.

"A simple misunderstanding," Ub assured him. "I'll clear it up."

But word was out, misleading though it was, and rumors spread quickly in the capital. When Kassander had turned down his proposition, Groth threatened him with nullification of the original Project Island purchase, citing the reasons he'd given Mr. Ub. A simple proposal of mutual advantage had transformed into an issue and possible scandal. The career and reputation of a deputy minister were in the cross hairs of lunatic fate.

"I'll be up a little late with something," he told his wife. "But don't worry. I'll be fresh to go in the morning to see you off."

Among the drafts on the table was a memo to his staff at the ministry. It advised them of the scurrilous nature of Groth's statements: Ub had sought to know if Essquibo stock were available, Groth was angry at not getting his way, Groth distorted Ub's request to gain revenge. Simple enough. No doubt they'd been gossiping on their own already, but this would provide an official response to give callers. He presented the same scenario in a follow-up letter to Dr. Kassander, augmenting his phone response. Groth must be seen as the deal-maker, or attempter, the driving force in the ill-fated proposal. Ub had also prepared a letter to his nominal superior, a brother-in-law of the king, adding a note of apology for any shadow, however slight and ephemeral, that might fall on the ministry. He took a much firmer tone, waxing indignant, in his complaint to Groth's commission in America, researched on the Internet by an assistant. If he were lucky, Ub thought, they'd provide a conciliatory reply he could use.

Still feeling agitated, he carried his drink from the library to the main parlor and the now-locked doors to the veranda. Pushing aside a curtain, he peered into the deep tropical night. He could see beyond the balustrade the sparse lights of the capital's nighttime commerce. It had been largely guided by his unseen hand, now employed in raising alcohol to his lips. Could it be, he wondered, that his judgment was slipping? To involve himself with someone like Groth—how could it have happened? Maybe it was age, a decline in faculties. He would have to be more careful. He needed to assess himself and his future, make some adjustments.

He tossed off his drink and returned to the library for a final check of his letters.

22.

Shots in the night.

Hawkins bolted upward in bed, hearing them clearly as sleep cleared off. Then, two or three seconds later, a final report.

Crouching instinctively in the dark, he looked out on the south coast. All quiet. He moved to a window looking out on the cove. No one around, Fong's building dark with the door closed, presumably locked. There were lights on the far point but that wasn't unusual. Someone was often up late there.

Hawkins ensured his door was locked and went back to bed.

* * *

Fong was at his door in the morning. It was very early, the sky a soft pink and the sun still blocked by the island's eastern rise. Roused from sleep again, Hawkins waited foggily for an explanation, but Fong himself was at a loss for words. Instead, he stood aside and pointed out toward the center of the cove, where a dark hump rose above the shallow water.

"Oh, no," Hawkins heard himself saying.

"I can't go out there myself," came Fong's distant voice. "You can understand, I'm sure, after the other time."

Hawkins nodded, then shook his head to clear it.

"We'll have to make a call," Fong continued, "but they'll want some information. A description."

They looked out over the peaceful water, the brutal flaw at its center.

"All right," Hawkins agreed, seeing no other way. "Let's have a look."

They walked down the beach to the point nearest the body. Hawkins waded in, receiving an unaccustomed shock from the chill dawn water. It settled into a vague sense of foreboding as he neared the dark form. A body, curled on its side on the sandy floor, but still dark at close look because—what was it? Unsure it was dead, Hawkins kept his distance as he waded around to the face, blurred below the water. An ape, a chimpanzee or something similar, and dead as could be. Though light was meager, Hawkins thought he saw a couple of fresh wounds and—could that be scar tissue, in a pattern on the chest? Hawkins slapped his arm, making sure he was awake, the situation existed, he was standing in the midst of it. Not finding himself back in bed, he turned away, waded back toward Fong on the beach. The caretaker was standing silently with arms folded, wanting no part of the adventure.

"It's an ape," Hawkins informed him.

After momentary surprise, Fong was visibly relieved.

"Did you hear some shots last night?" Hawkins asked.

But Fong shook his head.

"I slept very soundly. Catching up, you know."

"Yeah. Well, you better make the call. I can come on with the description."

"Do you think it's necessary? It's only an ape."

Hawkins pictured the wounds, the pattern of scar tissue.

"There's a little more involved, I think. We better get them out here."

Captain Rua and team arrived an hour and a half later. Hawkins saw them lingering as they passed the north end, talking with someone who'd emerged from the model. After some discussion, the group continued southward toward the spectacle. Fong stood at Hawkins's side. They could see now that it was Groth with the police.

"Relax, Mr. Fong," smiled Rua. "Your employer explained what has happened."

"Actually," said Hawkins, "we're not clear on that ourselves."

"Very simple," Rua replied glibly. "There was an intruder by the house, this animal. It was a threat to the people inside, so Mr. Groth shot it."

Groth nodded in agreement.

"But, captain," Hawkins said softly, "have you read my description of the body?"

Rua's expression stiffened.

"We will deal with that later, sir. As you can see, we are processing this and not leaving it for the refuse barge."

He turned to the other police and briskly gave orders. A bag for the body was laid out and Rua's men waded into the cove. They clearly found their task distasteful and were awkward handling the body. Captain Rua smiled at the onlookers.

"They are not trained for apes. You are getting special service today."

"Could they use some help?" Hawkins offered.

"Do not trouble yourself, sir. They are well enough paid."

It occurred to Hawkins that no one seemed curious as to why there was an ape of this size on the island. Fong wanted to avoid involvement, Groth was grateful he hadn't shot a human, and the police were content for now with removal. Well, he wasn't about to take on the issue himself. The acknowledged hermit would live and let live.

To the north, through a window of the model, Max stood watching as he waited for the coffee maker to finish. He'd awoken to Groth's voice nearby, excitedly talking to police about the shooting. They'd moved on by the time he was dressed, so he'd picked up the action with Susanna's binoculars. The body they were recovering was unconscionably decomposed for being only hours dead, or else it was some kind of animal. Max left the window and moved out to the veranda for a better look. As he began to raise the binoculars, he was alerted by his peripheral vision to several figures standing outside the boundary fence, watching the body recovery from the Essquibo side. Crouching back to the doorway, Max raised the binoculars and saw Hans Hanssen with one of his guards and the lab worker who'd kissed Hawkins by the boulders. She wore a brimmed hat and was indeed very pale, but she lacked the glow she'd shown in the moonlight. She had a pained expression, while Hans appeared angry, the guard at a loss. They never turned toward Max as their attention was riveted to the beach.

This must involve the project, Max thought. There's been some slip, a loss of control. Hans might be interested in that dalliance by the boulders. A talking point anyway, a contribution I can make. They'll need to tighten the screws now. I can help and get a bigger foot in the door. What's to lose?

Max retreated to have his morning coffee, any shame felt at spying on Traci and Hawkins eclipsed now by the prospect of gain.

23.

The commission chairman sat at his highly polished desk, a scattering of documents before him. Clouded light fell from the windows behind him, which overlooked tree-lined boulevards. The chairman, husky and genial, middle-aged, looked up and smiled as an elderly visitor poked his head in the doorway.

"Come on in, Phil. Glad you beat the rain."

Phil spryly entered and took a padded seat before the desk.

"Haven't been in town for a while. Wore the suit with the least holes."

The chairman laughed.

"You're always welcome here, holes or no."

Phil nodded.

"Thanks, Dave. But, ah, I guess there's some business. Right?"

"I'm afraid so. I don't mean to drag you out of retirement, but something's come up and, well, I decided I should get your input."

"My input? Sure, Dave. Anything I can do to help."

The chairman straightened, looked down at the papers on his desk.

"Albert Groth. You were his mentor, I believe."

Phil's eyes widened.

"Why, yes. But that was a long, long time ago."

"Before my time," Dave acknowledged. "But with the situation we have—a mess really, Albert at the center—I need to tap into your relationship with him."

"A mess? Albert? But he was always so scrupulous. No one more eager to please, at least where his standing was concerned, promotions and such. And he'd always been that way, it seems. He confided to me one night—we'd had a drink or two—that he'd been nicknamed "brown" or "little brown," short for "brown nose," by his old schoolmates. It went on less openly when he tried to become a professor, and I suppose with the state when he first started. But he's nonetheless tried to do everything right with the commission. He's been assigned as receiver as much as anyone, I think."

"Which brings us to the current problem. Bear with me, Phil."

Dave recounted the predicament of Gaville Associates, Groth's being assigned as receiver, his decision to focus on the Cove of Dreams development.

"He felt he needed to go there, try and turn it around somehow, be super-scrupulous."

Phil gave a tentative smile.

"Yes, that's Albert."

"Trouble is, he was due back long ago and," Dave nodded toward the documents, "it appears things have gone haywire."

He bent over his desk and selected a multi-paged letter.

"We've heard from an attorney for Essquibo Institute, the other outfit on the island. He says Albert tried to muscle them into selling an interest in their business, using corrupt local officials and bribery. They wouldn't go along and so Albert shot—yes, *shot*—a chimpanzee that was valuable in their research. There's a local police report attached."

Phil was open-mouthed but speechless.

"Then we have this letter from a deputy trade minister, name of Ub. He's 'most indignant,' he says, about Albert misrepresenting him for his—for Albert's—own gain."

"What do those ribbons mean?"

"Nothing. It's just the way they do things there."

Dave moved on to a legal document on long sheets of paper.

"This one has 'pain in the ass' written all over it. Someone named Zing Fong—yet another country involved—is suing everybody in sight for the unjust detention of his father, including Albert and Gaville for 'employee abuse.' Fong senior is apparently custodian at this Cove of Dreams. He was being held on some minor charge, later dropped, and Albert refused to pay the bail for him."

Phil's face was a mask of worry.

"Purely financial principles, I'm sure. Albert's enthusiasm could sometimes cloud his judgment. I did my best with him but—"

"Well, he was outside the box on this next one, I'll tell you, and it went through the governor's office "

Dave held up some hand-written sheets and a typed directive with familiar letterhead and bold signature. Phil waited apprehensively.

"It's from one Susanna Hoort. She and her husband have a house on order at this Cove of Dreams. They're living in the model till it's built. Our guy has seen fit to plant himself in the model with them, an extended stay now. Sounds like she's going nuts with him there. Complains about his personal habits—it gets pretty gross. Also his way of talking to her, obnoxious. She even says he's into, well, voyeurism."

"What No "

Dave stared grimly at the older man.

"There's more, of course. The other concerns of Gaville left unattended, Albert's duties as commissioner still on his colleagues' backs. But you can see where this is going."

Phil nodded reluctantly.

"I'm meeting Judge Richter for lunch. I want you to come with me, Phil. Richter remembers you, respects you, and knows about your connection to Albert. It'll make it easier for him to pull Albert off, assign a new receiver. Especially if you're the replacement."

Phil was alarmed.

"Me? But I'm retired And how could I do that to Albert?"

"It's for his good as much as anyone's. I could take it, of course, but that would look disciplinary to Albert, and giving it to another commissioner would crush his ego. You're the most gentle recourse, Phil, the one he can best live with later. And we have to get him out of *that place*. That's what he needs more than anything."

In the end, Phil was convinced. The two men left the office together, resigned to enter the drizzle that flecked the room's windows. A wall clock signaled the imminent lunch hour and, with it, the end of labored achievements for Albert Groth.

24.

Fong sat at the airport bar, time on his hands before the flight home. Hawkins had offered to see him off here, but Fong had said no. No sense his friend wasting a day. They shook hands on the pier, Hawkins handing Fong's luggage into the water taxi. It occurred to Fong that he should have kept one of those trade magazines Hawkins always gave him. They weren't of much interest on the island, but—well, the pharmacy house was all he had now. Something that could showcase their products, glorify them like those pipe fittings, it would have to be a help.

"Another drink, sir?" the bartender asked.

"No, I'm done."

He swung off the barstool, thinking he might call Hawkins, ask him to send one of the magazines to his address back home. Like jewels they were, Fong mused about the fittings.

The airport seemed much different from the last time he was here. All that tension when it should have felt welcoming. Today it was relaxed and airy, a scattering of casual travelers wandering about. No one to harass him, no pressure—just so he got the hell out. He strolled into a business services area near the arrival and departure gates. A plaque proclaimed it was courtesy of the Ministry of Commerce, with the name and ornate signature of the prince who headed it. Fong noted that one still had to pay to use the Internet connection.

"Cash only. Pay in tobacco shop."

Deciding he should email his daughter, he went to pay the fee.

Settled at the console and relaxed from alcohol, he slowly typed his message:

Greetings, Leti. How are you, I wonder? Fine I hope. You might be surprised by this message I'm sending you. No need, it's just I wanted to tell you something. I'm coming home. Not for a visit, to stay just briefly and then return to this place, but for good. You see, something happened with the company I was working for. They no longer own the property. The new owners do not require my services. So, I will be coming there and will work in our business. I think I can improve it so it is much more successful. Please do not worry about money for your education. I will be handling that, if not with the business then with something additional. Just pay attention to your studies so you qualify for university. I know you find chemistry boring but it can be important later, qualify you for things, so please study it for me. Well, I'll see you soon so we can talk some more then. My regards to Mother. Take care.

He sent it off and sat back in his chair, gazed into space above the wall of the cubicle. A part of his life was done, he realized, his residence in this country and his work on that strange island. Had there been some meaning to it beyond helping Leti? Those conversations with Hawkins, talk of the unknown, the void, potential in all the emptiness. He wished he'd had more education. Perhaps he should do more reading once he'd settled in back home.

25.

Dr. Kassander was examining Poobah in the EAU, occasionally dictating a change in regimen to Ana. She took notes on a clipboard while Jun, a guard, stood nearby.

"He's been acceptably calm lately, you say?"

"Yes. No real hostility since we lost Popeye. We've paired him with Chico on the exercise and there's been no problems."

"Hm. Well, let's just keep bringing him along metabolically. We'll see what direction we want to take later. We might try an incremental approach, give him another transgene, or—well, a totally different strategy."

He patted Poobah's shoulder.

"Back to your cage now, my friend."

He signaled to Jun, who came and led Poobah away.

"You're keeping an eye on the cage locks?"

"Yes," said Ana. "It seems it was just Popeye. No imitators."

Kassander nodded somberly.

"We've taken a blow. But that has to mean we work harder, more carefully."

"I'll do everything I can, doctor."

"I know you will, Ana."

As he left, the doctor passed Jun, who was dutifully checking cage locks. The guard waited a moment after the door closed, slowly smiled, then casually walked back to Ana at the examining table. She herself smiled but didn't turn at first.

"Now, what are you up to?" she asked.

"We are alone here, Ana."

"Alone, hey? I see quite a few eyes on us."

Jun glanced around at the animals. He was the youngest and handsomest of the guards, shiny waves of hair atop his deeply golden features. He and his comrades were imports from another, much larger group of islands.

"Let's visit the town, Ana. You should take a break from this."

"They might not be friendly there just now. What happened to Popeye, before that Mr. Tabor—they might be very suspicious, not want us around."

"So who knows? Just some police, some office people."

"No, word spreads fast in a small place. There's superstitions, fear. I wouldn't be comfortable, Jun."

He looked at the floor, disappointed. Ana touched his arm.

"We're in a special situation here," she said. "We can't just do what we want. Not right away, I mean."

Jun drew a breath as he looked up.

"We think we will be gone from here soon," he said. "Seems Hanssen is bringing in Europeans to replace us. To cover his ass with the company over Popeye."

"Oh, I'm sorry."

But Jun shook his head.

"When it happens, maybe it can be good for us, you know? I can take you from here to my country. We can have a life where no one can bother us."

Ana smiled sadly. He didn't know she'd achieved that *here*.

"But Jun, there are many details. Besides my work here, I have no status in your place. I don't have good papers. They might not even let me in."

"I could come for you in the outrigger boat, with my friends. We'll take you over the sea at night and sneak into my village by the inlet. No one would see us through the tall reeds."

Bemused, Ana gazed on his earnest expression, tenderly touched his face.

"My friend," she said, "what can I say to you?"

Outside, Dr. Kassander had paused in returning to his office. He lit a cigarette and walked more slowly to the east, toward the heliport, getting beyond the buildings and gaining a view of the sea. He considered its vastness, immutability, and the futility of his work in changing much of anything in the world. His wife in the distant homeland waited patiently for his return, just as she'd always waited in their dull, melancholy city for him to return from studies, then practice, then teaching, then research, all within the medieval strictures of their society. And now even here, in a place and time that had promised redemption, he was again sidetracked by the type of doltish bureaucrats that had been his bane. Disgusted, he flicked aside the cigarette. He'd do what he could to pick up the pieces, move on as he'd just advised Ana. Turning back toward the compound, he strode briskly to his meeting with Hans and Traci.

They were waiting for him in his office, surprisingly relaxed he thought. He sat behind his desk, moved some papers aside, removed his glasses.

"Poobah's fine," he smiled at Traci. Then, the smile fading, "I wish I could say the same about the state of our project." And to Hans, "Have you mentioned Hoort's remarks?"

"Yes. Traci bears them out, more or less, but there's something much more to it. An opportunity, perhaps a great one."

He looked to Traci, Dr. Kassander shifting to her also.

"I've been with Mr. Hawkins a number of times," she said in a clinical tone. "He's age 63 and appears to be in excellent physical health. Despite his solitary ways, he seems psychologically normal. I think he has reserve intelligence he can draw on. He's resourceful, and his judgment in moving here might well have been sound, based on inner knowledge of his own needs. He enjoys life and I believe he'd want to extend it."

Kassander's expression brightened. He reached to retrieve his glasses.

"And this assessment is not colored by, ah, personal involvement?"

"No," Traci replied calmly. "The opportunity Hans mentioned was *produced* by our 'personal involvement.' I am the reason he wishes to live longer than he would naturally."

"Hoort said she looked like a goddess out there," Hans injected, "the moonlight and all. Hawkins must think so, too."

"Well," Kassander grinned, "it's nice that others share our opinion."

He sat back and swivelled to one side, reflecting.

"He's a few years younger than the target population for marketing. Also not rich enough, but of course we won't be charging him. Ideally, assuming Popeye was a success, we should do full organ replacement and then the chromosome. The larger male chimp is primed as a donor, is he not?"

Traci nodded.

"Chuckles," she said.

"What?"

"That's his name, Chuckles."

"Maybe we can afford to ourselves," Hans proffered. "We seem to be back on track."

"Just so we stay focused," said Kassander. "There's much to be done. We need to know, Traci, how receptive Hawkins is to organ replacement. Strictly speaking, it needn't be done, though it would lengthen his use of the chromosome. Carefully feel him out on that. As always, there are ethics to maintain, even as we take some liberties. The human subject must know what he's getting into and, where there's a choice, the options must be explained."

Back in the EAU, Jun had left and Ana prepared to take the dogs out. She attached collars with leads to two but decided to take the third out separately. He hadn't been keeping up since a recent hormone experiment. Ana felt compassion for the animals, was aware it could become excessive, inappropriate, but wasn't worried about it. Her motivation in her work here—the need for it, closeness to colleagues, gratitude to Essquibo—guaranteed her loyalty to the requirements of the project. Jun was nice but, besides being younger, was proposing a type of existence that she'd long ago decided was fantasy.

Exiting the EAU, Ana and her charges walked to the hill on the southeast of the island. It was here that helicopters circled as they approached the heliport. Ana looked to the sea and then back over the compound, felt a warmth rise within her. Only about fifteen people, she thought, and not even all this small island, and yet it's the world for me. She felt the wind in her chestnut hair, the lab coat flutter on her compact body.

"Still," she said aloud, "it's nice to be noticed that way."

26.

The lone passenger in the water taxi, Hawkins gazed distractedly over the waves. He'd usually be charged with anticipation on this trip, looking forward to his first view of Lydia, its promise of a great day ahead. He'd grown accustomed to it already. But this time the crossing was different, a tentative venture that could easily prove fruitless. He hadn't been able to contact her, much less arrange their meeting. With the relationship they'd developed, it seemed reasonable for him to try to find her, or at least discover what had happened. He tried to envision possibilities, but found he somehow didn't know her well enough to guess very far. This strengthened his urge to search for her, as well as his sense that it was right.

The water taxi put in at its customary pier on the waterfront. Though Hawkins had left messages for Lydia via phone and email, she was nowhere in sight. He wasn't surprised. He strode past the waiting tricycles, one of which he'd normally board with Lydia, and headed on foot for the nearby city center.

Hawkins hadn't forgotten Traci in his concern for Lydia. His involvement with Traci, though, and what it could mean for him, was something separate and totally different from his friendship with Lydia. Because friendship, really, was as far as he could go with Lydia, no matter how intimate they were. There was his age, in addition to his basic nature, and

Lydia's needs that were also limited, subject to scheduling. It was something mature and in the traditional world. With Traci, however, there was something that challenged the usual boundaries on relationships and on living in general. It was totally outside the scope of his experience, of most people's probably, and he felt compelled to follow through. At least for now, with no reason not to. Would Lydia understand if she knew? She wouldn't like it, he thought, so it would have to affect their relationship. But at present that wasn't an issue since he didn't even know where she was. And he was deeply concerned about her, felt the need to find her, his involvement with Traci notwithstanding.

Hawkins walked through the city's commercial zone, eventually reaching the banks and government buildings at its core. He asked directions to the culture ministry and soon found it in a less imposing building. A young man struggling with a copy machine directed him to a woman who might be Lydia's supervisor. They talked in an open lounge area.

"Miss Coe is no longer with us. She was supposed to work with music programs, but she did very little. She only came in a few days."

"Have you heard from her since she came to work?"

"She sent a postcard from the Auckland airport. It simply said she resigned. Goodbye. Just like that."

Hawkins looked away, tried to focus. A small indoor fountain trickled nearby. The supervisor, about Hawkins's age, gave him an appraising look.

"You were close to Miss Coe?"

"I was on the B List," he managed. "We did B List business."

He thanked the woman and retraced his steps to the street. So Lydia was gone, he kept thinking, and without even telling him. There was obviously much more to it, but why didn't she let him know? Maybe he hadn't ever known her well at all. They'd been close, but that might've been just within a compartment of her life. The B List compartment, just as he'd impulsively told that woman. He was bothered by this thought, accelerated his pace to the trade ministry. He wanted to look into other of Lydia's compartments, vicariously become part of them, make better sense of his situation with her.

Perhaps noting his height and purposeful gait, the outside guards straightened as Hawkins reached the building. The inside guard greeted him but didn't pat him down, accepting his claim to be a friend of Mr. Ub. Hawkins made his way to the outer office, sitting by a potted palm while Ub finished with a trade representative. The deputy minister seemed surprised to see him, but affable.

"We haven't had occasion to meet lately," he commented.

"I'm afraid I haven't learned much about the project, Essquibo. That you don't already know from Captain Rua, I mean."

Ub waved dismissively.

"Don't bother with that, Mr. Hawkins. Apes in the water, what do we care? Just so they're not running loose in the capital."

He laughed, then suddenly sobered.

"Of course, you had that person out there, now thankfully recalled. We certainly don't need *his* type around here—a troublemaker. No, I'd say we've removed the real problem out on Project Island."

Hawkins let the point settle, restless to move on.

"I was wondering about Lydia," he said. "I haven't heard from her for some time and I haven't been able to contact her."

"Have you tried at her apartment?"

"No, not yet."

"It might be worth a try. I too haven't talked with her recently, and I suppose I had cause for concern. They called from the culture ministry and said she stopped coming to work. I had no explanation for them, I was very surprised. I hope she's all right."

"Would the police be any help?"

"No, I'm afraid not."

"But you must have some influence with them."

"Indirectly, yes. But they'd be no help on this. They don't look for 'missing persons,' only take reports. And there's Lydia's reputation we must think of."

"What about her relatives, her friends?"

Mr. Ub's expression brightened.

"Yes, she has two sisters she sees, and their children, her nieces and nephews. Here, I still have her emergency card."

He opened a desk drawer and picked through a card file, pulling a card out.

"One of them is here on the main island, the other would cost you a boat trip. Another one, that is. I'll give you the address of the close one."

He copied it onto a message slip.

"It's across the island by the resorts. She has a little store there, I think. You take the airport road but keep going past the turnoff. Your driver should know."

Hawkins took the slip.

"Thank you. There's no one here in town, though? Friends, maybe?"

"Lydia kept her personal life quite private, despite the role she had with the B List."

"I can appreciate that, though it makes things more of a mystery now."

"Yes, I agree."

Mr. Ub relaxed in his chair, appearing complacent to Hawkins, as if providing the address relieved him of cause for concern. He apparently didn't know about the postcard from Lydia's stopover.

"I suppose she might just be traveling," Hawkins ventured. "An impulsive getaway."

Mr. Ub looked dubious.

"Very unlike her, I'd say. Especially giving no notice at work, or to yourself for that matter. Correct?"

Hawkins nodded as if in thought.

"What about emigration? Did she ever express any—well, not plans exactly but, say, opinions about it?"

"Not to me," Ub responded. "But then, that doesn't mean much." He smiled. "People here don't talk openly about it, but I'm sure that—given the right opportunity, something feasible for them—many of our citizens would emigrate."

Hawkins discreetly feigned surprise.

"They don't like it here? The nice climate, the peace, the culture and traditions and all?"

"You can love your home and still want to leave it. The lure of another place that meets your needs. Especially as one grows older. You yourself, if I may say—"

"Yes, of course. I guess I should understand emigration."

"It's simply one of the choices we make in life, a choice made freely or in response to crisis. Some even see it as destiny."

His penetrating gaze unsettled Hawkins. Did Ub know more than he let on?

"I can't argue with that," Hawkins said.

"I appreciate your coming to our country," Ub resumed, "a successful businessman from a stable, powerful country. Also the responsible way you've conducted yourself here. You're certainly a 'best citizen' even without the pin "

Hawkins sensed he wanted to wrap things up.

"Thank you. And thanks for all you did for Lydia."

"You're most welcome."

Leaving the building, Hawkins had the feeling he'd been given the bum's rush. True, Ub had seen him without an appointment and there was business to get back to. But the official had not seemed to share his visitor's sense of urgency. Ub was ready to wash his hands not only of Project Island but, apparently, Lydia as well. Hawkins didn't understand this but he saw what it might mean. He was becoming isolated in his concern about Lydia, perhaps the last person for whom it was important that she be here. Others would simply accept that she'd disappeared. Traces of her existence would quickly fade away, life in the Kingdom going on as always. It would be as if they'd never met, never been as close as they had.

27.

Lydia arrived downtown and alighted from the city bus she'd taken. She was still getting used to wearing a coat, even lightweight, but today would be good practice. She was going to take a "whale watch" tour on her day off. It was still some distance to the hotel lobby where the tour began, but Lydia didn't mind the walk. It was good to be striding along here, a full adult again, after her week with her employer's children.

"Spare change, lady?" someone said.

"Help me out, ma'am?" said another.

She was getting better at navigating these stretches, but she'd take a different route on her return. It was nice enough here overall, but the last thing she needed was to be reminded of the world she'd left.

She noticed a disturbance ahead, slowed her pace a bit.

A crowd of mostly women was milling about outside a government building. A speaker was shouting into a megaphone from where she stood on a bench. She sounded angry but Lydia couldn't get her gist. Others were cheering, however, some with signs referring to a public law, a policy, and respect for domestic workers. Lydia noticed that the women were of various ethnicities, but the majority seemed to come from her part of the world.

"Come to join us, sister?"

It was a young woman in a windbreaker, some literature in her arm.

"No, I was just walking. I saw this so I stopped."

"It's about immigration policy, the injustice. You are familiar?"

"Injustice?"

"For domestic workers. The rule we cannot have our real professions. We are teachers, nurses, even doctors. But we must stay domestic workers because that's our visa."

She was a compatriot of the guards on Project Island, Lydia realized.

"Can you not go south, to the States?"

"That's very complicated, almost impossible. Don't you know that? That's why we're here. Are you just a tourist?"

"No, I work for a company."

"Oh, good for you. But can you still join our march today?"

"I'm sorry, I have an appointment."

"Well, here. Take a booklet. It's about our movement."

"I'm afraid I don't read your language."

"That's just the cover. The inside is English."

Lydia wished her well and continued on to the whale watch. Clearly, she thought, one could do worse than take the course she'd taken. She too was a sort of domestic worker, but her employment with the family was under the aegis of the Essquibo Institute. She'd chosen it over another option, as a stepping stone, with a much better prospect for mobility than the women in that crowd. It was good that they could meet at least, speak and vent their feelings.

28.

Hawkins approached a waiting tricycle and gave directions to the Lydia's building.

They moved out of the city center and through the commercial ring, then some shabby neighborhoods and vacant land, eventually arriving in the upscale residential area. Hawkins had the driver wait on the quiet street, which featured bowls of flowers hanging on the street lamps. He rang Lydia's bell in the building's small lobby but, as expected, received no response. He repeated the exercise, then tried the door to the stairs but found it locked. There was no one in sight around the building or nearby on the street. It was midday and growing hot; the buildings here were air-conditioned. Hawkins returned to the tricycle.

"Take me to the Neptune's Pride restaurant," he told the driver.

Arriving at their familiar haunt, he let the driver go and sat at a shaded table on the terrace. With Lydia he'd have gone inside, but he didn't want to get too comfortable now.

"An old-fashioned, sir?" asked a familiar waiter.

"Better make it a beer today. No, wait I'll have a whiskey sour."

Lydia's drink. As if she were there, a gesture. But everything pointed to her being gone, Hawkins realized, and with finality.

Perhaps the most he could hope for was to know why. The waiter came promptly with his drink, asked if he'd like to order food. Glancing over the menu, Hawkins asked for basil mussels with sweet ginger pineapple, a squid salad on the side. He smiled as he spoke, thinking it an order that Lydia might give.

"By the way," he added, "You know that lady I sometimes meet here?"

"Yes, sir. Very nice lady."

"I was wondering, has she been in here recently? Since the last time you saw us both?"

"No sir, I haven't seen her. Is there a problem?"

"No, no problem. I was just wondering if she's back from a trip."

The waiter smiled and went away. When he returned with the food, Hawkins re-ordered the beer he'd canceled earlier. He needed to adjust, he told himself, to understand that the little world he'd arranged here for himself was not his final destination. His meetings with Traci, her unique allure, and what she'd said about the project showed that his life was not in denouement. Though it didn't feel good now, Lydia's absence might just accommodate a new and better scheme of things. At the same time, munching this food in their meeting place, he retained a strong sense of her, a relationship happier than his previous ones, albeit less intense. He needed to make a smooth transition, keep Lydia in his heart as he moved forward into— what? He wasn't at all sure, really. But, with Lydia gone, he was more driven than ever to find out.

Finishing his meal, Hawkins asked the waiter to call him a cab. The trip to see Julia, Lydia's sister, would be wearing in a tricycle, especially in the midday heat after taking whiskey and beer. Hawkins was again reminded of his age, his stage in life, and moved to stay in the shade. He soon saw a boxy limo arrive in front of the restaurant.

The driver was familiar with the route and exited the city with unnecessary speed. There was very little traffic, especially after they passed the turnoff for the airport, the cluster of small businesses around the junction. Hawkins blinked at a flash of reflected sunlight from the sign of the Bad Gong restaurant. They moved into a countryside with shanties and a few struggling farms, stretches with sparse growth apparently useless. They passed a wetland area with children trying to catch things in the water. As they came to a gigantic hill of garbage the driver glanced back at Hawkins.

"Almost there," he said.

They arrived among the resorts that neighbored the wide sandy beaches of this district. There were cross streets again, the driver turning into what seemed the main commercial stretch.

"You will try the casino while you're here?"

"No, just the one stop. Then straight back."

The driver grunted, evidently bemused. He soon located Julia's store and got out for a smoke while Hawkins went inside. Small souvenirs and gift items, all quite cheap, were displayed throughout the interior. Hawkins at first wondered how anyone could make a living here, then noticed a teller window near the back festooned with lottery tickets, colorful and in various languages. There was also a chalk board with odds for boxing matches and a "game of the week," probably rugby. An old man with a soft drink was chatting and laughing with a teenage boy behind the grill. Hawkins was about to approach them when Julia herself appeared through the postcards and sunglasses. He explained who he was.

"Yes," she said, "Lydia mentioned you."

She looked younger than Lydia, hair cut shorter but strong facial similarity. She seemed less tall, but might have just been fuller figured. A different sort of life, different work could do that, Hawkins reflected.

"This is your store, then?"

"Yes, with my husband. That is my son." She nodded toward the lottery window. "We have two others, another son and a daughter."

It occurred again to Hawkins how little he'd actually known about Lydia.

"It seems maybe Lydia left the Kingdom," he said.

Julia was mute but held his gaze.

"I was wondering if you'd heard from her."

"Just one call. She's gone, yes, but she's okay."

Hawkins waited but she didn't volunteer more.

"Any idea why she left? When she's coming back, if she is?"

"She—" Julia stopped to think. "Lydia was disenchanted. Oh, not with you, or with anyone specially. She'd just gone a long time, not married—she just got tired of things here, with the place I mean. She had a feeling she had to get out. That's how I understand it."

"Think she'll be back?"

"I don't know. I'm sorry." She glanced toward the back of the store. "Wait, there's something I can give you. I'll be right back."

She returned with a key.

"It's for Lydia's apartment. She left it with me long ago. She said when she called to go and take what I wanted, that there wasn't much. You can use it if you want, see what you can find about her. She wouldn't mind, I think."

Hawkins was moved. Lydia was gone, but here was this kindness through her sister.

"I'll get it back to you," he promised.

The drive back to the city was oddly pleasant for Hawkins. Though Julia had essentially confirmed his fears, there was enough of Lydia in her way to soften the blow, to make it gracious. Then there was this key, turned now in his fingers as the nondescript fields slipped past. A trust between the two of them, now passed on to him. So he was still involved with Lydia after all.

They reached her building and Hawkins dismissed the driver, the cab fare grown quite high. The key was the type that opened both stairway and apartment doors. A strange, suggestive stillness hung in the air as he entered Lydia's abode, emphasizing her profound absence. The light, modern furniture sat as always, the bed was made in the bedroom, and many of her clothes remained. Hawkins could see, though, that many smaller items were missing, including decorations that would rarely ever move. A notable exception was a "Home Sweet Home" sign he'd once brought here in a lighter moment. As he stood in the waning light from outside, he noticed a blue ribbon draped over the sign and tied in several loose knots. Between the knots were three shiny objects. Moving closer, he saw that they were irregular in shape, reddish, metallic—copper pipe fittings Hawkins stood staring at the once-familiar objects, their proximity to the sign, and imagined Lydia arranging this. He knew where she'd gone now, he thought. Feeling a nostalgic warmth, he lifted the ribbon off the sign and carefully stored it in his pocket, the fittings still attached. This was all he'd take; Julia could have the rest. He'd mail her the key from the waterfront post office.

Hawkins took his time leaving the apartment, then walked for a while before flagging down a tricycle. The day's heat was lifting, the sky orange and fading to violet. He should return to

Project Island, he thought, but, since he'd have trouble getting the water taxi at this time anyway, he might as well have a look at Tuja's, a club Lydia had frequented. It was part of her life here; he'd make it part of his memory of her. His driver knew the way.

The city in the evening seemed to lack solidity, to take on a tepid liquid quality, pierced by shouts from unseen sources. Splashy neon signs identified the clubs, including Tuja's, which had added "What's Your Poison?" beneath its name. There weren't many customers when Hawkins first entered, but it filled up steadily as he had his first drink. He was having a beer at the bar but, with the people coming in, felt like something stronger. His mood was somehow celebratory, as if he'd had a successful day. He ordered a scotch-on-rocks, not knowing how they did the cocktails here. He thought about Lydia, but the texture of his thoughts grew thinner as he drank, giving way to fascination with Traci and their future. This hardly required thought at all. He had another scotch, which seemed rather weak, but rather than complain he just ordered another. He suddenly wondered if he should feel guilty, if it was wrong to Lydia for him to go ahead with Traci. He'd had it all sorted out before, but now he wasn't so sure. And yet maybe it didn't matter. Some things just had to happen.

"You want a date then, uncle?"

A heavily made-up young woman was talking to him, his vision blurred beyond her face. Another face came up beside hers, however—male and smirking, familiar somehow.

"Mr. Hawkins is too tired tonight," said Captain Rua. "He needs to come with us and have a sleep."

He was out of uniform, asking now about a hotel, but Hawkins could only shake his head. Rua and a companion took him by the arms and led him through the crowd, a ripple of laughter in their wake. They proceeded to a police car taken for personal use after hours. It would have to make one more official trip today.

The car pulled out for the drunk tank.

29.

Susanna sat at the bedroom window with her birdwatching binoculars. She was wearing her new swimsuit, a modest but stylish one-piece, and scanning the far side of the cove for a sign of Hawkins. She also ranged out to sea and back across the cove to the beach and properties. There was no sign of Hawkins but she sighted Fong inspecting the building materials that had been dumped on numbers 13 and 15. The new receiver had cleared construction of the house they'd ordered for number 14. Susanna was happy to be rid of Groth, feeling close to Max again without the obnoxious presence, but also still feeling the restive insatiability that had claimed her at puberty. The peace here didn't calm it, just gave it free rein. She now considered Fong as he adjusted a tarp over sacks of concrete.

"Nice enough body," she murmured, "but that mind-set, too much of a work thing."

She waited a while longer for Hawkins to show, then got up and stretched, liking the swimsuit's feel on her body. She knew she was slightly ungainly, but why should that matter when she was slim, and feminine, and willing to relate warmly with a quality man? She got along well at Max's side with the various people they met, those that mattered at least, her occasional forays simply ornaments on their successful life. Max had his own idea of success, of course, always wanting more, needing to *affirm* himself in his field as much as possible. And so here they were on this island, hiding and recuperating, establishing a resource for later. Well, it was part of being married to him, which wasn't all that bad.

She stepped into her sandals and clopped out to the stairway, descended to the ground floor of the model. Max was bent over his laptop at the dining table.

"Work or play?" she asked.

"Oh, let's see. Playing at work, I suppose. Sprucing up programs before I see Kassander."

"Hm," she intoned, glancing at a jumble on the screen. Max's work always bored her.

"Going for a swim?"

"Maybe." A hesitation. "Max, would this extend our stay here, your getting involved with Essquibo?"

He stopped pecking keys.

"I don't know. Not necessarily. We'll have to see what works out, if anything."

She moved her hand from the chair to his shoulder.

"And what works for *me?* You said it was just a season here—get acquainted with the retreat, move on. Back to the flow, the real people."

He covered her hand with his own.

"Darling, I know what I said. And I know I want the best for us, you especially." He smiled. "But you know, we do have a new house going up here. That's something else we have to attend to, anyway."

Susanna wasn't moved.

"That hairball said they put these up fast, almost as fast as that box for Fong."

"Well, we know better now than to trust Mr. Groth, don't we?"

She withdrew her hand.

"It's dull here, Max. We have to face that. Maybe not for you, with your number crunching or whatever, but I'm different. I have—"

She was struck suddenly by the earnestness in his face. She realized that, whatever her other needs, she needed him more than anyone. She returned her hand to him, caressing the side of his face.

"I think I'll swim now."

"Sure."

Instead of heading right to the water, however, Susanna walked down the beach to their home site. Fong would still be puttering around, she thought, and she could use his conversation, however vapid, to dilute the effect of Max's. Then she could lose herself in the cove, relax freed from guilt.

Fong was talking on his cell phone, however, sitting on some lumber with his back to Susanna as she approached. She waited a few moments, thinking the call might be brief.

"I'm very lucky to still have this job," Fong was saying. "If they hadn't removed Mr. Groth, he'd have fired me instead. Your lawsuit would've been disastrous for all of us. Your uncle can't save the business by himself, and Leti would never have the money for university."

Fong listened, Susanna a short distance behind him.

"No, Zing. You must drop the lawsuit. It's not on my behalf, no matter what the lawyer says. There's no guarantee of ever getting anything and everyone can be hurt, as I've said. Don't you have other prospects, maybe for a better job?"

Another interval, Fong grunting a couple of times.

"RV components, I don't know. Gas prices the way they are, that's probably why they're selling cheap. Still, it sounds better than the other thing—loans of credit ratings, did you say? Sounds very shaky. So, how were you going to finance that RV move?"

Susanna stepped away toward the water.

The sun was not yet at zenith and there were more clouds than usual, though still white and scattered. The water would be rather cool but still looked inviting as Susanna approached it. She wanted to be refreshed. It occurred to her that this view of the cove, its opening to the sea, was ideal and would always be theirs from the new house. Max chose well. It separated him from men who floundered in life. Still, with all he gave her and allowed her, she constantly felt the need to be renewed. She waded into the water, eventually reaching a depth for swimming. The water invading her swimsuit provided its usual ephemeral thrill. She moved with her long, awkward strokes toward the mouth of the cove, not intending to exit but to hover there, at the gateway to riskier waters. That was her method, she realized; she was basically a flirt. She actually went farther than flirting but never really risked anything. She always pulled back before anyone could claim her from Max.

Treading water between the points, Susanna sighted Hawkins on the beach, walking from the landing area toward Fong. He'd arrived on the water taxi, she supposed. Given the time of day, he must have been on the big island overnight, probably with that woman. Susanna recalled her binocular view of Lydia, the other woman's graceful walk as she visited Hawkins. Susanna again felt the rising envy and dismissed it with inner anger as being ridiculous. She watched the two men on the beach proceed to the prefab, perhaps seeking liquid refreshment. She began swimming toward the southern point, Hawkins's cottage, but slowed and stopped before touching bottom. She was on track to what she'd done the other time, she realized, but she didn't want that. It wouldn't work and, however brief, there would be the humiliation. Maybe more this time—him just back from that woman and drinking away with Fong, her in the modest swimsuit bought to appease his shyness.

Susanna reversed course, swimming across the cove's mouth to the narrowing beach before the model.

Max wasn't around, apparently on the errand he'd mentioned. Susanna shed her swimsuit and had a shower, using far more soap than was necessary. She needed to be cleansed of something deep, she thought—her whole self. She needed to start life anew, as the birds did with each short flight, each call or chirping. A purified present, affirmation—I exist She sighed as the warm water rinsed her, felt innocent in its flow despite her desires. Later she took her time drying, then nestled in her lilac robe since Hawkins's was returned. Wanting to clear her mind and drowsy from the shower, she stretched out on the bed and quickly dozed off.

The sound of a door slam awakened her. Still cozy on the bed, she heard Max at the fridge and liquor cabinet, preparing an early drink. Celebrating, perhaps? She warily raised herself, gained her slippers, and descended the stairs.

"Total washout," Max informed her. "They're somehow back on track with the initial strategy. No resources now for alternatives." He shrugged. "I don't know, I guess they found another smart ape."

Susanna had to turn away, hide her involuntary grin.

Thank you, ape, she thought.

30.

The magnate and his doctor walked from the 18th green to the clubhouse, their well-tipped caddies retreating to store the clubs. The weather had been iffy when they started out, but the sky had cleared nicely and signaled a pleasant, cool evening. They took a table on the terrace.

"Bring us each another in fifteen minutes," the magnate told the server who brought their drinks. He was an exacting, pre-emptive man who left as little as possible to chance. He lit a cigar and looked out over the grounds, his face assuming its business expression. It was time for some news, good or bad.

"So, do we have a green light, then?"

The doctor, deferential as he'd been on the course, leaned forward.

"Essentially, yes. If you're sure you want to go ahead."

The magnate laughed.

"What other direction is there at my age, except down?"

"You're healthy enough for 71, and there are risks inherent in any operation."

"Surely the procedure is pretty well vetted by now."

"Yes, they've done an exacting sequence of trials. Only a final test run remaining. Dr. Kassander has the highest reputation for skill and precautions."

"On balance, then, for a man of my means, it's a simple choice. Five or ten years of decline into senility, or centuries of life in better shape then now."

"Barring accidents, yes."

"Being rich gives you incentive to be careful."

The doctor hesitated, swirling his drink.

"There will be documents to sign, a lawyer or two to see, perhaps a financial person."

"Sooner the better. Do it before I die!"

"You're absolutely sure, then? I have responsibility as your physician."

The magnate sat back and smiled.

"Don't worry, doc. I'm still of sound mind."

The doctor considered telling him that he wouldn't be alone, that there would be two other paying clients at the project with him. He decided not to, not just now. The magnate would find out soon enough anyway, and he might think the doctor was encouraging him. That would hardly be appropriate, the doctor thought, since he doubted he'd be seeking the procedure for himself later. For that matter, he doubted that Dr. Kassander would.

It wasn't just being rich that made you careful. So did being wise.

31.

Traci led Hawkins to the compound from the rough growth above the south shore boulders. A crescent moon hung in the sky, raising a lesser glow from Traci's features. Hawkins was now used to her gratuitous mutters, though he wondered what other odd qualities she had, what secrets. It was somehow part of her appeal, he thought, though it was what she'd revealed, promised, that was the ineluctable force in their relationship.

They approached the EAU, entered with Traci's key.

"They like visitors," she assured him.

He followed her in, caught the odor of animals, sensed their stares from the shadows. The light was stronger toward the back, whence metallic noises could be heard. Traci hastened ahead to have a look.

"Ana "

"I'm just finishing up. We'd let the mice cages slide."

Hawkins came up and Traci introduced them. In their lab coats, Hawkins thought, Traci looked thin compared to Ana, though the assistant was normal build.

"He's here to meet Chuckles," Traci explained.

Ana nodded knowingly.

"Sort of a layman's appraisal," Traci added.

"Yes. Well, I'll just be going."

As she left them, Hawkins noticed, Ana glanced back with something beyond curiosity, beyond professionalism. A flicker of something he couldn't fathom. Was she remembering Tabor, his fate?

"Anyway," said Traci, "this is Chuckles over here."

The larger male chimp had been moved to Popeye's old cage, its lock thoroughly cleaned and tested.

"He's kept separated from the others?"

"The other young male, Chico, got the chromosome as a control. It shouldn't affect him much, but if it makes him feisty with Chastity we don't want Chuckles involved. We want him perfectly primed for transplants."

"Chastity is a female chimp?"

Traci nodded with a little smile.

"They came as a lot. There's no plans for her at present."

Hawkins stood before the cage, rusty in his appraiser's role. The cottage had been ordered new, and he hadn't checked out a vehicle or shipment of pipe fittings for a long time. Now here he was, negotiating organs. He eyed Chuckles warily, the chimp responding in kind. Did he somehow know what was on the table? There was no hint of amusement or even friendliness from the chimp, despite his name. He hung back from the bars as if sensing a predator before him, his eyes never leaving those of Hawkins. His existence would end, of course, if the full procedure were performed. He couldn't know the specifics but sensed that a great brutality awaited him, Hawkins thought. He viewed the ape's chest while touching his own, considering those specifics, the incredible operation this was leading to. He felt slightly sickened and Chuckles shifted in his cage—relaxing? Hawkins turned away.

"Tabor did this?"

"Viewed his donor? I'm not sure. But in his case, with his age, there wasn't much choice. And he only got individual genes."

Hawkins nodded.

"Your husband and you, of course no surgery."

Traci looked startled, recovered.

"It was a much different situation. We weren't market-oriented."

She sat back against a table.

"Cyril had lost a sister and his father to illness by the time we met as students. His first interest had been immunology but more exposure to science led him to bio-technology. We met as research assistants, worked together through many long nights, meeting deadlines for a professor. Cyril made a discovery that could facilitate chromosome construction. The professor claimed it as his own, but that's par for the course in universities. Cyril wanted to take things further, get into therapeutical applications, but the professor was against it. He didn't like controversy, he was comfortable as he was. There was a national initiative at the time and Cyril was able to get public funding, to extend the research on his own. Those were good days for us, for a while."

She hesitated, drifting in recollection.

"What happened?" Hawkins probed.

"Well, news got out on what we were doing, the potential for life extension. Some people didn't like it—'tampering with nature,' 'playing God,' all that. Our old professor joined in, disowned us. In government they raised social and economic issues, always some kind of fear to weigh against us. The upshot was we lost our funding, had to move from a modern lab to a closed middle school, a disastrous lack of materials and controls."

"And yet, you kept going?"

"Cyril did. He improvised, unwilling to see the work stopped. I found it difficult—not having the precision, the normal number of tests and trials, the confidence. I wound up in a supportive role, almost an observer. We were short on test animals, didn't even have a primate at the crucial juncture, so Cyril had to experiment on himself."

Hawkins winced.

"That must have been really hard for you."

"I guess I should have stopped him, but the work had come to be everything for us. Anyway, the chromosome created an imbalance in Cyril, his nervous system unable to handle the alterations in metabolism. He had trouble sleeping and was often depressed. He was able to make an improved chromosome, but was hung up on the substitution process, so I asked him to give it to me using a carrier virus. I had to contribute something at that point, to make things better in some way. I guess I also might have sensed Cyril going down, that his work might be lost with him forever. As it happened, he died the night after the procedure. Went out for a walk and perished in the park from stroke."

"I'm sorry."

"Thank you. His work has gone on, though. He lives for me through the work. It hasn't been easy reconstructing things—deciphering his notes, converting to well-equipped methodology. But this facility has been perfect for it, just about. There's the marketability thing, the combined strategy with the surgery, but I've accepted that. Pure science or general benefit to humanity doesn't sell. I certainly learned that with Cyril. It takes people like Dr. Kassander and Hans to have a real chance for progress."

The mention of surgery reminded Hawkins of himself and Chuckles.

"This surgery, say I didn't have it. I just got the chromosome. I'd basically have the same results you did?"

"No, the benefits would be proportionate to your general condition, primarily your stage of life. However, um—" She thought a moment. "You'd avoid the minor flaws that existed in the version Cyril gave me."

"That glow in the moonlight wouldn't be a flaw for a lot of people."

Traci smiled.

"Indirect effect of increased immunity, masked in the current model. Not many people would want those baby monologues, though, would they? Neural configuration, corrected with our improved processes. And one more, one we decided not to change."

There was a note of eagerness in her voice. Hawkins braced himself.

"Stay there," she said.

She moved down the aisle a little and undid her lab coat, glancing back over her shoulder at him. She was wearing a light sleeveless top and shorts underneath. When she turned to face Hawkins, he saw why she'd appeared scrawny next to Ana. Though indeed slender, Traci's body was perfectly proportioned with near-perfect muscle and skin tone, no excess fat or settling of frame. It was the body of a girl in her early teens.

"Reverse aging?" asked Hawkins.

"Not exactly. Reversion in body form, distribution of tissues. Not in size, though, the skeletal dimensions."

"Are you still going back?"

Traci laughed.

"No, I'm aging. But very, very slowly."
"Will this happen to me?"

Traci glanced back at Chuckles.

"Just with his help. Otherwise you'll look like you did at 50 to 55."

"Did that happen with Tabor?"

"No, he was past his potential for reversion, besides only getting transgenes. His benefit, what should have been his benefit, was the slow aging. He could have added decades to his natural life. Without Chuckles, it'd be your main benefit, too. Though your pickup will be around a century." Traci paused. "Of course, with the full procedure—with Chuckles—you'd be like me "

She held out her arms, smiling an invitation.

"What's your projected lifespan?" Hawkins inquired.

"Accidents aside, more then half a millennium."

Hawkins smiled and nodded, let it all sink in. He was amazed by the small woman before him, her gameness and dedication, her offer to him of a superior life with her. It raised their relationship to something more than human, he thought. At the same time, weighing 100 years against 500, he didn't feel compelled to look past that first century—not if it required having Chuckles stuffed into him. The first 100 years would be the best anyway, he thought.

His appraisal skills were returning, he thought further.

32.

Mr. Ub stood on the veranda of his mansion with Senator Rua, father of the police captain. They held cocktails with tinkling ice and viewed the city and waterfront in the colors of sunset. The rooms behind them were quiet, the senator having stopped by unexpectedly. He was well-dressed like his host, but shorter and with less girth.

"From here it's just like always," he remarked, "yet so much has changed."

"Yes," agreed Ub, "a different world from when we started out."

"Ah, the world. You'd know that better than me. The contact with so many foreigners now, from all over, their competing interests."

"Yes, it's an effort keeping them straight, styling communication. They have their different values, cultures and such. All different ways of doing business."

"Quite a challenge. But, you've always been up to it. I know the minister holds you in high esteem, always has."

Ub nodded, not wishing to discuss the do-nothing royal who was technically his superior. The senator no doubt sensed this, shifting his stance and sipping, preparing to raise the reason for his visit.

"So," he said, "how do you think Sparky's doing on that situation?"

The childhood nickname of Captain Rua had followed him to adulthood.

"Project Island?" Mr. Ub queried.

"Yes. He was hoping to do well on it, gain credit toward promotion. You know how young men are. They want their expensive toys."

"Well, he's doing fine, I suppose. As much as can be done, anyway. Nothing much has happened since that ape washed up."

Senator Rua studied his drink.

"I understand there were marks on it, scars from an operation, similar to those found on the Australian."

"Evidently, yes. Though we no longer had Tabor's body to compare."

"Nor those missing parts, internal organs."

"No."

The senator appeared thoughtful. Mr. Ub wondered where this was going.

"Sparky mentioned an alert from Interior, a change of title out there. You heard?"

"Yes, between the two companies. It seemed of little consequence. The project people bought most of the bankrupt development. The new receiver is apparently more competent than the one who shot the ape."

The senator nodded.

"The world is full of oafs. Unfortunate he saw fit to slander you, taint your reputation."

Ub was inwardly disturbed.

"Do you think I'm tainted?"

"Of course not, not personally. In the public eye, though, there could be questions as to why he chose to involve you. The mere flaunting of local clout seems so crude, unnecessary. Though if a man is incompetent, well, I suppose there are no limits."

"So what is implied then, in the 'public eye?'"

Rua shrugged.

"Perhaps some knowledge of their operations, of something valuable. Enough to entice an honorable man to involve himself with a sleazy go-between."

"And how would I have gained such knowledge? *Insider* knowledge, after all?"

"Well, there are still those missing organs, nobody explaining—"

Rua gestured in the air, as if at a loss. Mr. Ub now felt wronged.

"We've done everything we can to straighten that out. Your own son is witness to our efforts. I've worked closely with him. Anyone who wants to make such baseless accusations is as bad as the idiot who started them "

The senator smiled and gripped Ub's shoulder.

"Relax, my friend. No one doubts you, not those who know you. These are idle rumors you should know about, that's all. So you can be ready, not be bothered if you happen to hear them elsewhere."

Mr. Ub allowed himself to be placated. He shouldn't become too upset, he knew, or it might suggest guilt. And there was much he honestly didn't know. If only that moron Groth hadn't come by that day. Then he could be purely honest in his protestations.

An ocean and a continent away, the object of Ub's ire was phoning his old mentor. Groth had been drinking, though the large stein on his night stand was now empty. He was sitting up in bed, his laptop before him, its screen the room's only illumination.

"It's rather late, Albert," Phil informed him.

"Yeah, but I gotta know something."

"And what might that be?"

Groth tried to collect his thoughts, remember some terminology.

"I been bringing up files, including on Gaville, and I seen you made a sale on that Cove of Dreams thing."

"Yes, that's true, Albert. The Essquibo Institute bought all remaining properties, 25 of an original 27, as I recall."

"Yeah, right. But what—I mean, how could you do that, Phil? You didn't sell short or nothing. They coulda had the whole island for less before Gaville even got there."

"They've apparently had an influx of investment capital. Something sparked a strong interest in their work there. Having most of the island gives them better security, also more room if they need it later."

"Security, right. Nobody shooting their chimps now." Groth's tone was sulky.

"Now, Albert. We need to put some things behind us. Remember?"

"Yeah. Yeah, I know. But say, Phil?"

"Yes?"

"You sure nobody got nothing back on that sale you did, Cove of Dreams?"

Phil cleared his throat.

"I think we'd better get some sleep, Albert. It really is very late."

"But what about it? Was there, you know—"

"Good night, Albert."

The connection was broken, Groth's hellos not bringing Phil back.

* * *

Senator and Captain Rua sat in conference in the older man's office. The father had lit a cigarette and paused in thought, smoke curling around him before a backdrop of framed photographs. Edgy in a guest chair, his son awaited his feedback.

"So you don't think your man just lost him. He just never appeared."

"He must have gone in the middle of the night. Killed time somewhere before his flight. There's that strip by the turnoff."

"You're sure that's him on the manifest?"

"Yes, diplomatic passport."

"And the wife was already gone."

"Traveling in California, the servants said. They were closing up the house. He left instructions, promised to send them their pay."

The senator sighed deeply.

"No doubt his resignation will also come." A hesitation. "I've known Ub a long time, always a faithful ally. I didn't think you'd discover anything, really. I was just settling doubts."

Captain Rua looked down, giving his father free rein.

"I think we can assume it has to do with Project Island," the senator resumed. "The events out there and his interest in them, that Groth fellow's story, and—wasn't there an aide of his who also took off?"

"Yes, Lydia Coe. She handled the B List before it was banned."

"Hm. So she would have connections on the island. And the list was stopped because of incidents connected to Essquibo. She and Ub were close, I believe, longtime associates. It would take money to make people disappear like that, big money, and a strong desire to conceal something."

"They're not a publicly traded company. We checked."

"No, of course not. They'd never want to be scrutinized. At least not until later, when they've succeeded here, when they have what they need to make the *really* big money"

"Then they pull out?"

"Maybe, maybe not. One thing's for sure: we'll never see any of that money."

"What about taxation?"

"Thanks to Mr. Ub, the island is autonomous. They pay fees for defense and emergency services, and for the refuse barge. That's all we get from them."

They were silent a moment.

"They might just fail, anyway," the captain ventured.

"Unlikely. The investors appear to have full confidence."

But then the senator's face lit up, piquing his son's curiosity.

"Your investigation is still open, is it not? The missing organs, the ape with scars, the connections to Essquibo?"

"Officially, yes. But—" The son gave a helpless gesture.

"Never mind. All that matters is you have access to them, to the project. Difficult, perhaps, but potentially a way to discover this resource they have, this source of extreme wealth. It's too bad for our country, unable to benefit from a discovery on its own soil. But we're also citizens of the world, Sparky, individuals like those foreigners out there, and we are family. There's no reason we shouldn't benefit even if our country cannot."

Captain Rua nodded. A loyal son, he'd accommodate his father. The vision of riches didn't make it any harder.

33.

The helicopter bringing the new team of guards arrived about midday. There were five of them, including a sergeant to relieve Hans of some supervisory duties. The helicopter remained on the pad to remove the outgoing guards from the project.

Aware of the transition, Ana came out of the synthesis lab and discreetly watched from a distance. She found herself put off by the voices and mannerisms of the new arrivals. Their brusque militarism stirred unpleasant memories of her own repressive culture. Jun and his colleagues had tempered their role with a relaxed Pacific mood. This new group would require adjustment by her, perhaps avoidance at first, however necessary they were.

Ana walked between the buildings to the area behind the compound, where she and Jun would sometimes meet and talk. The trees leading to the cove were in the distance. She moved parallel to them, toward the southern coast, regaining a view of the approach to the heliport. She didn't want to miss Jun's departure. As she came to the rough growth above the shore with the boulders, she saw a man picking his way through them, departing.

Mr. Hawkins, she thought, our next test subject. He didn't see her. She considered calling out, decided not to. It didn't seem right, somehow.

A strange, empty feeling came over Ana. Here was another unconnected person, suddenly here with her in this isolated spot, unaware of her as she'd been of him. Yet they shared involvement in such a tremendous project. That was something to be protected, a reason to protect their roles, not call out. But did it justify their ongoing aloneness? Was their sad lack of partners really something good, truly prerequisite to roles that helped achieve so much?

She turned away from the retreating figure, thought of Jun.

"I can take you from here to my country," he'd said.

She pictured for a moment going over the sea by outrigger, sneaking into his village behind tall reeds. How utterly crazy, and yet she suddenly felt a pull toward the compound, more resolved than ever not to miss his departure.

She quickly walked back, taking a direction to the front of the compound.

She lingered outside the EAU, spotting Jun and the others as they left the residential unit with their packs. Since they were encumbered, she easily intercepted them on the path to the heliport. She thanked them for their work but the others kept moving when Jun stopped. Hans and the new sergeant were watching from the compound.

"What can you do?" he shrugged.

She offered her hand. He gripped it gently.

"Until we meet again," he said.

"I admire you," Ana replied.

He smiled and turned to follow his comrades. Ana retreated to the compound, away from Hans and the sergeant, and waited in the shade of a tree for Jun to vanish.

34.

The fence separating the western end of Project Island from the original Essquibo property had been removed. The Hoorts' new house at 14 Cove of Dreams was near completion. The couple was expected to vacate the model, now Essquibo property, as soon as possible. Fong's prefab was gone, as was Fong himself, his visa becoming void once his employer sold out. Hawkins was free to cross through the trees to the project's compound, having become a key participant there. While he'd declined the Chuckles option, disappointing Dr. Kassander, a great breakthrough was anticipated with the infusion of the chromosome.

"So you're satisfied with the stability?" asked Ana.

"Yes," Traci replied, "it's constructed as well as it can be. Just keep its environment as steady as possible until the procedure. The subject's too, when he checks in."

"Dr. Kassander will want a final examination."

"There won't be any problem. He's exceeded standards for a subject his age."

"We had him on so few supplements, even less than the chimps."

"He didn't need much. He's had Cyril's catalyst, so he's fine."

"Hm, okay."

Ana returned to her microscope. Traci almost kidded her about worrying too much, but held back. Ana had been a bit down since the guards were changed, Hans bringing in a more aggressive group. She'd apparently been sweet on the one who'd helped exercise the animals. No doubt she felt the loss, here on this small island, despite the challenging work that kept them busy. It was something Traci could relate to, of course, after Cyril. On the other hand, she now had this bond with Hawkins with its promise of love and common cause for their extended futures. Much of what she'd personally lost with Cyril would be restored. Her shortcomings in the mistakes—the disaster—would be vindicated, more or less. This feeling might be cold, Traci thought, but things were much more complicated for her than for someone like Ana, who could just track down her lover when they were through here.

"Are his forms all in?" Traci asked.

"Mr. Hawkins? Yes, but he was sketchy. For the emergency contact he only had an email address. Lydia something."

"That's all right. After Tabor, Dr. Kassander's not looking to talk with relatives."

An ocean away, in a chilly city, the Lydia in question was meeting with her employer. She'd been working as a nanny and normally had evenings free, but the father had called from his office and asked her to stay. They were in his study now. The children and their mother were elsewhere in the house, a part-time cook preparing dinner.

"You've been wonderful with the children," the father said, "but there's been a development. Something that could improve your situation. Here in America, I mean."

He referred to the continent, Lydia being north of her eventual goal. She didn't comment but listened attentively.

"I was contacted by the Institute today. There's been some real progress at the facility back in your homeland. It's apparently due to a new team member, someone they say you know, a Mr. Hawkins."

"Merv?"

"Fellow with a cabin there, lives by himself."

"Yes, Merv Hawkins. But how—he was in copper pipe fittings, retired—"

The man shrugged.

"All I know is he's with us now, though he likely won't remain on Project Island. He'll probably be returning to his old haunts, south of our border here. Given your—well, acquaintance with him—everyone might be better off if you lived and worked in the same area. Two team members, mutually supportive. If you're willing, of course."

Deep within her, Lydia felt wild excitement rising.

"You can arrange this?"

"Essquibo can. As of now, I mean, with this outlook for success."

"I don't know what to say. But yes, I'm agreeable. This is so sudden—"

The man smiled.

"It just seems that way. All great accomplishments do. But they actually develop over time, with great effort, expense, patience, and risk. That's the Essquibo view, anyway."

"Yes, and of course I agree with it."

As she had with Mr. Ub, then Dr. Kassander, Lydia listened to the details of her impending transfer. She'd been moving farther and farther from her past, the needs and aspirations of her youth, but she now felt she was returning to something. A man she cared for, empowerment, the ability to do things and travel as she wished, even visit the Kingdom. She thought she knew now why people were attracted to the Essquibo Institute, became committed to it. It made the possible *happen*. It was bold.

* * *

Hawkins lay in a narrow bed in a room of the Operations Unit. There was a larger bed against the opposite wall, heavy duty and equipped with restraints. The recovery spot for the chimps, he guessed. Tabor had likely lain where he himself was now, surfacing from a sedative of some sort. Dr. Kassander's need for control, Hawkins reflected. His own decision-making stopped with his declining the Chuckles option. After that it was all following instructions, following orders. He supposed it was for the best, but felt a rising urge to return to his cottage, his own little corner of the Cove of Dreams.

Not that he hadn't been dreaming *here*, after the infusion. As he was coming up, he experienced a mélange of fragmentary scenes, himself at the center but getting no special notice. On city streets, in lobbies and hallways of large buildings, in train or subway cars, there were plenty of people but always a sense of something lost, missing, or undone. In a lecture room, a dingy restaurant, or waiting for something on hard chairs, he had companions yet none he could name now. There was an overwhelming sense of mediocrity. Finding himself in this plain, utilitarian room, recalling Traci and the procedure, Hawkins had been greatly relieved.

He had to chuckle, thinking how it had come to this. All those years with the business, the clumsy dates, his foggy understanding of life. Then he stumbles in here and gets lucky.

He wondered how Lydia was, how she was getting along, and found he really cared.

35.

Capt. Rua and a junior officer, both in civilian clothes, had stopped at Tuja's before proceeding to the night's business. They had drinks at the bar and ordered a second round, but left before finishing as if called away on an emergency. They were actually just putting in an appearance in case alibis were later needed.

They drove a short distance to the apartment of a grocer's son who was also a reserve officer. There were two other men in the cramped residence, both perhaps still in their teens. Cigarette smoke filled the air as Rua's colleague pulled down the shades.

"You can vouch for these two?" Rua asked the reserve.

"Yes. And they're good on the water. From the resort coast."

The captain grunted and cleared space on the available table. He unrolled a hand-drawn map he'd carried in from the car. It was an enlargement of Project Island as it appeared on the police map of the Kingdom, with added details reflecting development by the purchasers.

"We know the pier is here," Rua pointed out, "and we know the houses on these two points, but the rest is approximate. You will have to judge what is the main office, or the main laboratory, and be very silent getting in."

"Hambo is good at breaking locks," said the reserve. "He's at the casino now. We could perhaps fetch him."

Capt. Rua considered for a moment.

"No, he's too awkward, not serious enough. I don't want someone blowing this." He looked back at the map. "Now, our plan is to get in and get out without being seen. There are guards but they're just store cops, drinking and chasing lady workers. Just don't act like Hambo and they won't even notice you."

Nobody laughed, though Rua's colleague cut a smile.

"We want laptops or hard drives," Rua continued, "paper records if they look important. But only take what you can easily carry."

"We'll be operating from offshore," his colleague explained.

"Yes," said Rua. "The launch will have lights out as we land in the dinghy. Not at the pier, of course. Beneath this rise, the least visible point." He straightened and looked at each of the men. "We need to use extreme caution. Do not hurry but keep moving. And later, of course, absolute secrecy. You will all be amply rewarded."

By the time they left the night was well along. Music and drinking owned the streets, subsiding as they approached the dock and police launch. It would be quite late when they got to the island. They'd settle in a spot of maximum advantage, Rua thought, and go in to strike at the quietest time. Even the latest workers would be done for the day, busy with other things if not asleep. And not much was needed, after all, just a little information. It should be easy.

36.

Shots in the night.

Hawkins, back in his cottage, raised himself on an elbow and listened. There was more than one gun this time. After the firing there were shouts in European accents. The new guards, one closer than the others.

As the voices subsided, Hawkins got up in the dark and did his inspection. He saw nothing unusual from the windows and so returned to bed.

* * *

In the morning, as Hawkins moved toward kitchen and coffee maker, the gentle light and lapping of surf brought to mind the other dawn after a shooting. Fong had knocked at about this time, with the remains of Popeye in the cove behind him. Well, he wasn't around to knock today, poor guy, having been canned. But then, as he handled the coffee maker, Hawkins was nagged by this thought, as if maybe he should take a look anyway out of respect for the caretaker. It's crazy, he told himself, but what the hell. He had more time than ever now.

As he discovered, there was in fact another form in the middle of the cove.

Dutifully wading out to the rumpled mass, Hawkins was warmed by a sense of communion with the familiar. Though the water was chill and dark, the light indirect as it filtered over the eastern rise, he was sharing a ritual with Fong and his former, pre-chromosome, self. He felt confident and accepting, with none of the trepidation he'd felt on approaching the dead Popeye. He could handle this creature, he was sure, whatever it was.

He found it was an inflatable dinghy, partially deflated from a couple of bullet holes. It was marked with a simplified crest of the Kingdom and "Nat. Police Marine Ops." Looking around, Hawkins saw no bodies or other objects in the vicinity. The beach was peaceful, as was the land beyond it, the Hoorts not stirring from their new home, number 14. Seeing he was on his own, Hawkins awkwardly dragged the dinghy toward the beach. He assumed the police would want to reclaim their property, not let it drift back out to sea.

Following earlier procedures, he called the police and reached Captain Rua.

"Mr. Hawkins? Thank you but we know already about the intrusion. Mr. Hanssen and Mr. Hoort called when it happened. We've been delayed slightly in responding."

The shots, Hawkins thought, and those voices.

"This is something else, Captain."

"Oh?"

Hawkins described his find in the cove, Rua not responding, waiting Hawkins out until there was nothing more he could say.

"So, did you want to pick it up then, or what?"

"Yes, well, I'll tell you what we should do on this, Mr. Hawkins. I greatly appreciate you notifying us and I'd like to ask for further assistance, if you don't mind. What I would like is, please compress the craft as best you can and please store it in a secure place on your property. We will retrieve it when we come to investigate the, ah, intrusion. That will be later today. Can you handle this for us as a citizen, Mr. Hawkins?"

"Yeah, I think so."

"Good. And by the way, please do not tell anyone about this, okay? At least for now. We don't want to compromise our investigation. You know, about who stole it and such."

"Okay, sure. I understand."

"Thank you very much, sir. We'll be there in a little while."

About an hour and a quarter later, two men came walking along the beach to where Hawkins stood waiting with the Hoorts, who had just gotten up. Neither of the men was Captain Rua, though one wore a stiffly starched uniform similar to the captain's. The other, larger man was in a short-sleeve rugby shirt with "Hambo" over a number 7 on the back. He also wore a crinkly-brimmed canvas hat, sandals, and denim shorts with a "Special Deputy" badge pinned to them. The regular officer explained that Captain Rua and an assistant were investigating in the project compound, that he and his partner would join them when they finished in the Cove. The Hoorts and Hawkins must be interviewed separately, he said, so they should please return to their respective houses. He then entered number 14 with the Hoorts, leaving Hawkins with the casual special deputy.

"That it?" asked Hambo, indicating Hawkins's cottage.

"Yes," the owner replied, unsure how to address the other man.

Hambo strode off briskly on his own. Hawkins noticed he was carrying a brown paper bag with items of some weight in it. Hawkins hurried to catch up.

"You got the package for us, right?" Hambo called back.

"Right. It's on the patio."

The visitor quickly found the dinghy, removed the plastic furniture that partially concealed it, and dragged it off the patio toward the outer shore. He laid it out so the markings were clear, then retrieved his bag from the patio. He took out a small can of paint or primer and was soon brushing a generous coat over the markings. Only when he was well along did he look up at Hawkins.

"We have to decommission it," he stated. "Prevent impersonation."

Hawkins nodded dubiously. A bullet-riddled dinghy seemed a poor resource for impersonating police. It also appeared that the coating over the markings was corrosive, completely obliterating the dinghy's pedigree. As the special deputy stepped back to inspect his work, Hawkins asked if he'd like something to drink.

"Beer if you got it," Hambo replied.

By the time Hawkins brought back the bottles, his supposed interviewer was bundling the dinghy with a roll of wire from his paper bag. The wire was copper, Hawkins noted, though of suspect quality. Hambo pulled and tied the wire with impressive strength.

"So," Hawkins said as they drank on the shaded patio, "you have another job also?"

His guest grunted.

"Security at the casino. Cheap pay."

"It's nice you can get some extra work."

Hambo laughed.

"Dirty work. They want to keep their uniforms clean."

He drained his bottle and went to get the dinghy, hoisted it on his shoulder and carried it off down the beach. He slowed as he approached number 14, waited as the door opened and the regular officer came out, taking his leave from the Hoorts. The police walked off together and Hawkins rejoined his neighbors.

"Not much of an interview," Max commented. "I just repeated my phone call, basically. Shots and shouts."

"He asked about the places we've been," Susanna added. "The famous cities."

"Seemed like he was killing time," said Max. "How did yours go?"

"Similar," Hawkins replied. "Nothing much to it."

Elsewhere on the island, Captain Rua and another officer were interviewing the Essquibo employees. Rua himself handled the professionals and their assistants, while the other officer debriefed the guards and met with kitchen and maintenance staff.

"They came from off the east end of the island," Hans explained, "below the hill for minimum visibility. Swimming or in small craft, main boat offshore, lights out. We think two got past the heliport, proceeded to the office or lab units. We don't think they got in."

"There was information of value there?" Rua inquired.

"It's *all* of value to *us*, of course. But yes, people with the right technical knowledge could profit from stealing our research."

"It's an area of much interest? There is great public demand?"

"You might say so, but right now we're only in the experimental stage."

Rua couldn't press the point; it wasn't his purpose here. That effort had been made and botched. Now he was on damage control, functioning in a way directly opposite to what his official role demanded. Rather than trying to identify the intruders, the planning behind the raid, his goal was to conceal any link to the department, himself, and of course his father. The irony didn't amuse him, given the disaster that failure would bring, and his unusually grave manner seemed to impress those he questioned. Here was true dedication, perhaps they thought.

"As with the others," he said to Ana, "I must ask if you have any knowledge, any suspicion even, about who these intruders were."

She hesitated, looking away to a corner of the room.

"You mean any possibility? Even remote?"

Rua felt his eyes open, quickly dropped the lids.

"Yes."

Ana gave a little smile.

"I'm sure there was nothing to it but—well, one of the guards, the ones who were here before, he and I would talk sometimes. You know, while working, and—"

She reddened a bit, searching for words.

"Yes, go on."

He listened professionally, a sphinx in khaki, as Ana related her chaste relationship with Jun. She was amused anew by Jun's vow to return for her, but Rua maintained his solemn demeanor. He'd been working to appear curious and astute, but now without effort absorbed Ana's story, appropriated it. Success for the day was at hand, he saw.

With the arrival of the investigators from the cove, Rua commenced a search for physical clues. He told his men to scour the area by the work buildings, as well as the route to shore past the heliport. He asked the Essquibo people to stay clear of where his men were searching. He himself circulated along the search area, ready to ensure that any discovery was handled right. One of the officers disappeared over the hill, descending toward the shore, while Rua kept an eye on Hambo, picking through weeds near the heliport. There suddenly came a call from the fourth officer, working near the synthesis lab.

"Captain, I've got it "

Rua affected calm as he strode to where the officer beckoned, a clump of brush next to an isolated tree. The discovery was a large wrench usable for breaking door locks, government issue. Rua glanced back and saw Hambo approaching curiously.

"Bag this object and put weeds around it so its shape doesn't show," the special deputy was ordered. "Then take it to the boat and stay there. Guard everything until we arrive."

The finder of the wrench went to get the searcher on the shore, who'd found a cigarette lighter and a washed-up shoe. Judging that the remaining shoe was in the water and wouldn't be of added value, Rua ended the search and said they were finished on the island. The three policemen were walking toward the compound's exit when Hans and Dr. Kassander came out of the office and lunchroom building. The policemen halted.

"We've completed our investigation," said Captain Rua. "We appreciate your cooperation and that of your staff. Please thank them for us."

"I will," said Dr. Kassander, "certainly. And we appreciate your thorough response. You clearly understand our concern. Were you able to determine anything, if I may ask?"

"We're taking some evidence back for analysis—articles left on the shore, some possible body fluids on weeds. But based on our interviews, I have a preliminary conclusion. I don't think your project is in danger, doctor. This seems to be an affair of the heart, a former guard from here coming to see the assistant lab lady."

"Ana?"

"Yes. She herself is not at fault, of course. I don't think she's in danger, but perhaps one of your guards can watch her for a while."

"We'll do that. Does everything end here, then?"

"For you, I think yes. We still have this evidence to process, and there's the matter of foreign nationals invading our territory. I will have to speak to our foreign minister."

"Well, we certainly appreciate your efforts. Thank you again, captain."

"You're most welcome."

* * *

Hawkins sat with Max on the Hoorts' veranda, the sun dipping low as they had cocktails and viewed the cove, the sea beyond it. Behind them were the sounds of Susanna preparing a light dinner. Max had related his afternoon call to Hans, the apparent conclusion drawn from the day's investigation. Hawkins had listened with tightly set lips.

"Seems a little far-fetched," said Max, "doesn't it?"

Hawkins shrugged.

"People in love, they can do crazy things."

"Hm. I think it had to do with their project. They must really have something there. I had something to offer on other approaches but they turned me down cold, at least Kassander."

"Well, I suppose time will tell."

"Yes. Too bad we won't see it through. We have to be leaving soon or Susanna will leave without me. You'll still be here though, I suppose. Do you still feel quite attached—perhaps committed—to this place?" A sly smile began.

He knows about Traci, Hawkins thought. That's all right. Secrets are just a bother.

"I don't know," he replied. "It's a big world out there, and I've been feeling bigger myself lately. More whole."

Max reflected on this, sipping his drink, while Hawkins gazed over the water and Susanna tossed a salad inside.

37.

In her room in the residential unit, in the haze of shallow sleep, Traci would revisit phases of her experience with Cyril. There were versions of the phases, nuanced by factors beyond her control, but they all pointed to her inevitable widowhood. Her dreams were steps to Cyril's doom and yet subconsciously she clung to them. They were her contact with him.

"You'd better sleep," she said, "don't you think?"

He was puzzling over his notes and reference books, his microscope at arm's length amid a scattering of slides. He didn't respond.

"Take it up tomorrow. A fresh look. I can stay with it awhile."

She leaned close to him and stroked his hair, tousled and needing a wash. His face was lined, especially around the eyes, his complexion sallow.

"Limited cell accommodation," he said, "the requirement for undersizing. If it could only be overcome. We could do so much more, still cover the risks."

"Darling, all you can do is prioritize."

He scowled.

"Prioritization favors the banal."

She hugged him from behind, pressing her face to his, seeing what she loved in him. It was the briefest warmth, however, because the scene changed and it was she herself at the work bench, testing formulas for preparatory nutrients, seeking a catalyst to facilitate replication. Cyril was standing nearby, intently examining a dog.

"It's looking good except for 20a," she said, "the mushroom. Can we do without it? You know the doctors won't like this many herbals, anyway."

"Won't like herbals?" he answered in mock surprise. "My, my. Since when do we care what the doctors like? Let them reread their Hippocratic oath."

He never looked up from the dog, but the scene again changed and he was noiselessly shouting, exasperated, the night dark through the windows behind him. She was trying to comfort him, her hands raised, but all that would work was to agree with him, to nod yes, yes, desperately agree that he knew what he was doing and she supported him.

Traci half-woke, let the tension ease in existential mists. Did it really happen? Am I in that life now? Where is here? But there were good times too, came the saving thought, presenting at once herself and Cyril on the lawns by a college stream, studying. So far they were from the realities of funding, conflicting ideologies, self-interest of health-care industries. Another season and they were in a pub by the fireplace, joking friends getting tipsy. But not she and Cyril, walking now in town, by the sea, stealing moments of intimacy, expressions of their spontaneous love. And the visit to her parents, that first time, so clear now at the table, then her parents talking later as they would.

"He seems nice but quite shy," says her mother. "Not adjusted."

"Serious type," her father proffers.

The images evaporated and she saw her darkened room, faint cracks of light around door and window. The familiar sense of loss encroached, one that would work its way back to Cyril, his essence, and beyond that to herself, her lost identity—her natural, pre-engineered self. She felt an impulse to resist, not give in this time. She was who she was, here and now, and Cyril's work lived on. It was good and great. She'd never give it up. She'd go to it now, she decided, go to Hawkins, purify her past in the glory of Cyril's legacy.

Donning the spare lab coat she used as a robe, Traci slipped out of her room and the unit. She deliberately passed the guard staying close to Ana. It was better than being discovered farther out, and her glow didn't show so much in the lights.

"Everything all right, doctor?"

"Yes, I couldn't sleep. Just taking a little walk."

"Be careful."

Traci made her way westward, toward the stand of trees that preceded the old Cove of Dreams development. She turned more to the south, toward Hawkins's end, and was soon through the trees with the point before her. The night was clear, as usual, the sea the only sound, and a sudden memory loomed as she sighted her destination.

"You did it " she saw herself saying, hunched over a sedated mouse. "Resistant to all pathogens "

He reacted with an expression, one she hadn't seen on him since their schooldays: positively beaming, luminous, all traces of strain and bitterness gone.

She now looked at her hands, luminous also—Cyril's gift—and ahead of her that expression, growing in this man who shared the gift with her. She'd seen it since the procedure, part of his innate understanding of their superiority, their post-banality lives. She took a deep breath, refreshed by the night air, the power of the sea, and with slow, deliberate steps approached the cottage.

* * *

They lay in each other's arms, the glow from her body lighting the contours of his face, the edges of each of his features. He was still a bit stunned, as he'd been when she appeared at the screen, and when she'd dropped her ersatz robe to reveal her full body. He was fully accepting, though, knowing at some deep level what she herself never questioned: they were lovers of a higher creation, refinements beyond all the world had known.

"I guess I can ask you now," he smiled. "That little *sotto voce*, the low talking that runs on. What exactly are you saying? Do you know?"

"Yes, I know," she teased. "It's been recorded."

"So, what is it?"

"Well, it's—" She hesitated. "It's Latin. Names of organisms I had to memorize at college. I'd be lying in the grass, or in a nook in the library."

"All still in there, huh?" He tapped her temple.

"The names, yes. But that's all it is, the little *sotto voce*." She laughed. "I hope you're not disappointed."

"I can live with it. I can live with anything now."

Traci wasn't sure how long they slept then, but she woke with a sense that the sky would soon be lightening. Hawkins lay heavily beside her, seeming massive though actually of rangy build. His breathing was slow and deep. Traci sat up, mentally preparing to leave. Hawkins didn't stir. She spoke his name but there was still no response.

"Merv, I have to get back."

He mumbled something.

"What? I have to go, Merv. Can you hear me?"

"Cut copper pipe with hacksaw or copper tube cutter. Both make satisfactory cut but tube cutter ensures square cut. Use jig or miter box when cutting with hacksaw."

"What?"

"Helps ensure square cut. Make jig from wooden board or block with vee notch to hold pipe in place. Slot in jig will guide saw at right angles to vee notch—"

He became unintelligible. Traci eased herself back and off the bed, stepped softly to where her lab coat lay, slipped it on. She peered for a time into the darkness containing Hawkins, but no parting comment seemed appropriate.

As she made her way along the Cove of Dreams, back toward the trees and the compound, she couldn't avoid the contrast between Cyril and Hawkins. The extremity in her husband's life and efforts, his cause, was a stark backdrop to the casual confidence, almost insouciance, shown by her new lover. But it's an unfair comparison, she realized. Hawkins is a *beneficiary* of Cyril's work as I myself am, which is what Cyril intended. In furthering his work, and now sharing the joy of its results, I'm promoting progress. I'm a catalyst for Cyril's success, like the nutrient formula he found.

Sighting the Hoorts' house, she recalled a comment made by Hans.

The man in there called me a goddess, she thought. But goddess of what? Extended life? Romantic sleeps on tropical islands? Or—yes, maybe just copper pipe fittings.

Traci smiled and went on through the trees.

38.

"Actually," said Dr. Kassander into the phone, "we have good accommodations here on the island now. There's a furnished three-bedroom on the property we annexed."

"Vacant?" the attorney inquired.

"Yes, and complete with beach. A warm, gentle cove."

"The associates will love that."

"I'm sure, and you might enjoy a dip yourself."

"I'll be doing most of the work, I'm afraid. I'm giving them a treat before things get busy. That and they should see the project, know what they're working with."

"Of course."

"There's not much more than one day's work, really, but we'll stay for two or three. Let them unwind, make sure we don't miss anything."

"We'll be at your disposal. Anything I can do, just let me know."

The attorney paused. Kassander heard papers rustling.

"Your last test subject, the partial procedure."

"Mr. Hawkins?"

"Yes. He owns one of the lots not titled to Essquibo. One of the two?"

"Yes, I believe that's the case."

"Hm, too bad. Better for us if he were renting."

"Oh? How's that?"

"Well, we really won't want him around when things start opening up—the press, publicity and such. He's not a representative client, only getting the chromosome without the surgery."

"Yes, he's mostly Traci's accomplishment."

"Plus he didn't pay. But there's also the human test-subject issue."

"You think that would be a problem? I mean practically?"

"The press might jump on it, draw parallels with things in the past. Unsavory things. I don't want to worry you. You're well insulated legally. But the financial effects, well—"

"What can we do?"

Papers rustled again on the attorney's end.

"I'll be looking into it. In the meantime, don't cite Hawkins as a success any more than you have to. The less attention he gets the better. Then, once you've done something with a paying client getting the full procedure, make that your showcase work. Trumpet it."

"All right," Dr. Kassander agreed. "We'll do that."

"Good. We're moving ahead rapidly now, doctor. Essquibo will expand on the same scale as your success there. You and your colleagues should be very proud."

"Thank you. We have an excellent team."

39.

There was activity around number 1 Cove of Dreams, the former model that had been vacant awhile. Hawkins learned from Max that a team of lawyers working for Essquibo had moved in. They would deal with patents, marketing rights, and corporate development necessitated by the project, and with protecting the Institute against litigation.

"I can well understand that part," Max asserted.

"How many of them are there?"

"I counted four, three men and a woman, all quite young except one of the men."

Later there were noises from the cove, childlike shouts, and Hawkins saw three of the lawyers splashing about on the northern side. Another man, probably the fourth lawyer, came walking down the beach in tee shirt, trunks, and sandals. He was met by Max, who directed him to Hawkins's cottage after a brief exchange. The man resumed his walk while Hawkins waited by the door.

"Mr. Hawkins?"

"Yes."

"Beau Jerome, from Thierry, Bates, and Welles."

He was tall and rather husky, with red hair atop a high forehead, earnest eyes, very light skin and freckled. Pure country, Hawkins thought, yet he's a lawyer. They shook hands.

"Something to drink?"

"Yes, thanks. Whatever's handy."

Hawkins got them each a calimansi juice. He knew he should cooperate with whatever was going on. He was part of the family, more or less, as far as Essquibo was concerned. He hadn't the faintest idea what he'd actually do, however.

"I guess you're pretty well settled," said Jerome. "It looks quite comfortable here."

"I like it."

They were in the living room, sunshine and shouts filtering through the screens.

"We won't disturb this paradise long. We're only here a few days on legal matters concerning the project. As you know, I believe, it's at an advanced stage now."

"Yes, of course."

"And you've been a big part of it."

Hawkins sipped his juice.

"Are you all right with the follow-up?" asked Jerome. "The checkups and such?"

"Sure, no problem."

"Good. We want to be sure you're thriving, and also that the procedure was problem-free." He hesitated. "You should stay with our doctors for a while, Mr. Hawkins, for anything that comes up. They're familiar with your new condition and, frankly, you just can't trust outsiders. There are people out there, strongly motivated, who'd like nothing better than to steal this discovery. They can be very unscrupulous. I understand there was actually an attack on this island by such a group."

"I thought that was a love affair, a former guard trying to carry off a lab worker."

Jerome laughed sarcastically, looking toward the window.

"Pure cover-up, someone's bull running loose." Another hesitation. "They failed but we can't assume that's the end of it. There are others out there more sophisticated. Word will spread through the medical community, with the potential for profit obvious to all. This island is likely to stay a target."

Hawkins listened to cavorting young lawyers, recalled shots in the night, then Traci's luminescence. It's true, he thought, the island is special.

"If you wanted off for a while," said Jerome, "or for good, we could facilitate things for you. Say back to the West Coast, your home area. We have our associates there, you'd have continuity of service, medical and all."

"I wasn't planning to leave, actually."

"Sure," Jerome smiled. "We just want you to know that, in case your 'new self' starts feeling footloose, it's okay with us. You're not tied to this island. There's just that caveat for a while on the medical, and a need for caution with people approaching you."

The attorney left his card. He was Hawkins's contact with Essquibo, he said, from now on. The people on the island were there for technical work only. Hawkins asked no questions, not wanting further complications. He watched Jerome walk off.

Hawkins stood for a while letting his mind settle, absorbing the lawyer's visit. Slowly he walked through to the game room. He picked a cue off the rack, balanced it in his hands, put it back. He looked out over the patio. The noise from the young lawyers had stopped. It was very still, it seemed, the stillness inviting action, a reaction on his part to Jerome. He wasn't, after all, his old retired self. He was his "new self," as the lawyer had put it, with greater potential for action, and therefore choices to make. At the very least, he should reread Lydia's email.

It had appeared a few days before. Hawkins had opted not to react, shelved it mentally, feeling he had enough to process with Traci and his new self. Now, however, he felt different and brought the message up on his laptop:

Hello Merv, I don't know what to say. Disappearing like that, to your eyes I mean, I'm sorry about the confusion. I wanted to tell you. I couldn't. I heard you were looking for me. It warmed my heart but made me feel bad for you too. The thing is, it all has to do with the company, there on the island. I've been told you're also in the group/network whatever now. So it's okay that you know they helped me get here, around where you used to live. I had to leave the Kingdom, for many reasons. We can talk about it in person some day, I hope. I mean soon. For now I want you to know that I'm okay, I have a nice job and place to live, and I love you and miss you.

Hawkins set the laptop on the coffee table, sat back and viewed the message from afar. He'd come to this place, 27 Cove of Dreams, Project Island, to be isolated from complications and involvements in the world, things that had mostly never worked for him. Yet now here he was, at the center of a major world development, his two best relationships with women occurring at the same time. He reflected on the irony but saw no deeper meaning. Those were simply the facts of his situation, what he had to handle. And he *could* handle them, he thought, being the new person he was. It was inevitable. Challenges were less daunting when your resources increased, opportunities more accessible.

An extra hundred years, he thought. Amazing. Yet looking into them all he saw was Traci—a beautiful life with her, yes, but nothing more. What exactly would he do? Maybe it didn't matter. Just having the time might be enough, especially with her. When he finally died though, looking as old as people can, Traci would still be fairly young, another 400 years to go. What would he be to her then, or after the next century? No one else would remember him so why should she? And of course she'd have other relationships, layers of experience over the dusty myth of himself. Time is a tricky thing to play with, Hawkins thought.

He retrieved his laptop from the coffee table. He read Lydia's email again and decided he should reply. It had been several days already. He typed:

Great to hear from you. Don't worry about the disappearing. I got a close-up look at the Kingdom out of it, the high and the low. Your sister is nice. She lent me a key to your place so I went and snooped around, looking for clues. I found the pipe fittings on the Home Sweet Home sign. I somehow guessed from it where you are, maybe just hoping. Anyway, it's true I'm involved with the project or company people. Details at another time. I have a lot to think about just now, what's happening here and you over there, the future etc. So I'll be in touch then, okay? I love you too.

He sent it off. Later, his laptop put away, Hawkins thought about his talk with Beau Jerome. What the lawyer had hinted at, suggested really, meshed nicely with what Lydia seemed to want. Maybe it would be for the best, given those lifespan issues with Traci. Of course, he was fixed to outlive Lydia, but maybe she could just get the chromosome to even things out. Hawkins smiled at his mental manipulations. He really was becoming an Essquibo person. He'd better watch out. He wanted to keep some Merv Hawkins in his great new self.

But as he thought this, rising to go outside, the image came to mind of Traci in the night, her unearthly glow and power. Fantastic, he thought. Perhaps irresistible.

40.

Traci and Dr. Kassander were having coffee together in the lunchroom of the Essquibo compound. There was no one else in sight, no sound except the air conditioning. He brought out his cigarettes and offered her one. She accepted and he lit them both up.

"It'll be do-it-yourself for lunch also, I'm afraid," said Kassander.

"They'll still be tied up? All day, you think?"

"I certainly hope not, but it's clearly more than a quick dusting."

Hans had detailed the kitchen and maintenance workers to number 1 Cove of Dreams to prepare the house for clients arriving that night. The visiting lawyers had left it in well-used condition, Hans explained, more like abused. No guards could be spared for the clean-up due to current security needs.

"What time are the subjects arriving?" Traci asked.

"Nine-thirty, flight conditions allowing. We'll get them right to bed and leave a staff person, apprise them as a group about this time tomorrow."

"Three at once. Quite a change in our operations."

"We must keep them in successive stages. Any delay in the lead subject's treatment means corresponding delays for the other subjects. No leap-frogging."

"Safety first. And less strain on us, less chance of error. Optimal conditions."

Kassander smiled.

"I increasingly count myself fortunate to have you as a colleague."

Traci returned the smile, raising her cigarette for a draw. She knew there could never be anything personal between them. However close they worked professionally, he and Hans regarded her as a freak, she believed. It might be different if her chromosome weren't flawed.

"Where in the sequence is the female subject?" she asked.

Kassander refocused, looking past her toward the kitchen.

"I have her second. I wasn't expecting a woman this early, but it will certainly help with marketing. So I see no reason to delay."

"Perhaps an 'Adam and Eve' motif when the story is leaked?"

Kassander almost laughed.

"Certainly not. Enough of that will follow by itself. Anyway, I've decided on an earlier leak after the first subject's transplants, to preempt any exposés lurking out there."

Traci looked at him in surprise.

"That'll put some pressure on."

"I'm sure you and Ana can handle it. Plus, success in the spotlight will maximize marketing potential. Of course, we'll tighten security as needed so we can work in peace."

Traci nodded, tapped ash from her cigarette.

"I expect Mr. Hawkins will fade as a credential for our program," Kassander went on. "His infusion got results in our network, this trio of clients arriving, but we'll be playing to a much bigger audience now. Successes with these three—complete, age-specific procedures—will essentially establish the industry." He shrugged. "Essquibo's industry."

Traci looked at him, tried to picture their work as an industry.

"Of course," she said, "the infusion by itself will be a secondary—uh, product."

"Of course," Kassander agreed. "But we know humanity, don't we? Its proclivity to deny mortality, to procrastinate, even in the most vital decisions and actions? Hence our primary focus: the full-service regimen, to be demonstrated on tonight's arrivals. There's a real beauty, I think, in the way things are turning out. A sort of scientific destiny."

The helicopter bringing the clients arrived on time, spoiling the starry sky over Project Island. It's approach was seen by Hawkins and the Hoorts from the couple's veranda. This was Max and Susanna's last full day on the island, perhaps for a long time, so they were savoring its reality with their only neighbor. Max had invited Hans but the Essquibo man was too busy. Hawkins would return in the morning to see the couple off.

"They must be working late at the project," Max said as the chopper passed.

"I haven't seen it around for a while," Hawkins observed.

"Well, they had those disruptions, the dead ape and those rascals invading. But I guess it's back to business as usual now."

"Yes." A hesitation. "Usual."

Hawkins gazed over the darkened cove toward the opening to the sea, searching for what exactly was usual, what the concept meant to him now.

"Care for a nightcap?"

"I don't want to keep you up, you must still have packing—"

"No, we're fine," Susanna spoke up. "Please stay for one more."

Max went to mix the drinks. Susanna, who was sitting between the men, leaned toward Hawkins and spoke quietly.

"I've been meaning to apologize for that first day. I had to say something to you before we left. I'm ashamed of the way I acted, how I bothered you that day."

"You don't have to—"

"No, let me finish. I'd like to be able to say there's something in my past, some experience, that makes me that way. But there isn't. I've always been that way, at least after childhood. Something in my nature, deep inside. Something in the genes."

"Genes," Hawkins repeated, "I can understand genes." But she meant in the usual sense, he reflected. She's back in the world of the usual. "Well, for sure you don't have to apologize then," he said. "We can't control our genes. Everybody knows that."

Susanna smiled.

"Max has accepted it. That's part of the love between us. I'm happy if you accept it, too. I want to feel we're the best of friends after I leave here."

"Sure, no doubt about it."

She quickly kissed his cheek.

"I think the drinks are coming," he added.

Susanna laughed and sat back. Max rejoined them and the evening wound to a close, the departing helicopter foreshadowing the Hoorts' own exit. As they were finishing their drinks, they saw the lights go on throughout number 1, figures moving in and out, an occasional raised voice piercing the night. Hawkins took his leave and returned to his cottage. When he looked out before getting into bed, he saw that all the lights were off at numbers 1 and 14.

Hawkins was up early next day to help the Hoorts move out. The golf cart used by Fong had devolved to them, so Hawkins used it to move their things to the pier. There was no activity at number 1 as he passed it, though he sensed its occupation.

And something else. He wouldn't have noticed it in the past, or he'd dismiss it as silly, but now he felt a danger of some sort, something ominous. He knew he wanted nothing to do with the people in there.

After the Hoorts had left on the water taxi, Hawkins checked the locks at number 14. He'd offered to keep an eye on things to supplement Captain Rua's services. Finding all was secure, he decided he could use a swim after his early morning labors. He returned to his cottage and was soon stroking through waves off the southern coast of the island. As he was gaining the familiar sense of isolation and peace for which he'd come to the island, another helicopter bore down in the project's approach pattern, its noise dancing off the waves around him. A flicker of irritation passed through Hawkins. He watched the craft pass around the hill and then settled into a more vigorous swim. He felt a sense of purpose, though with unclear focus. Perhaps he simply wanted or needed some purpose for his reclaimed strength.

As Hawkins was getting his lunch later, feeling relaxed after his swim, he heard a ruckus of some sort in the direction of the Hoorts' house. Peering out through the screens, he was startled to see several apes running about between the trees and the beach. Traci's assistant and one of the guards were chasing after them, trying to grab the apes' trailing leads. Hawkins glanced at some fruit on his table, thinking it might calm the apes, but then remembered these were experimental animals, no doubt on special diets. Thinking he should help, he stepped out from the cottage. This distracted the apes and slowed them down. Ana and the guard each gained a lead, with another guard coming through the trees to assist. Order was restored.

"We just had a couple come in," Ana explained, "so we tried walking them with Chico. It got out of hand, of course. We'll have to go back to two at a time."

"These are for a couple patients, these new ones?"

"Clients, yes. They're staying down the beach. But there are three, actually."

"Oh." He hesitated. "How's Chuckles doing?"

Ana gave a coy smile.

"Well, I can't say he misses you."

"Same here." He looked down the beach toward number 1. "Guess he'll be getting involved with someone else now."

"Could be. We haven't matched them up yet. There's a lady client, so she might be getting Chastity instead."

Hawkins nodded.

"They'll be having that meeting, like I had with Chuckles?"

Ana hesitated, perhaps remembering the look she gave him that night, a sort of warning it had seemed.

"Maybe. We'll see. Whatever seems best for each client, his or her procedure."

Later, in the synthesis lab, Ana raised the question with Traci.

"Mr. Hawkins brought it up," she added.

"Hm. Well, they can't take a lesser alternative, like he did. Any backing down and it's a wasted trip, not to mention the big deposit they paid. We'd be doing them a service not to let that happen. Let's avoid the eye-to-eye, just drop it. I'm sure Dr. Kassander will agree. Strongly."

Ana resumed her work without responding. Traci wondered if she'd sounded brusque. She admired Ana's compassion, but thought herself compassionate also. She simply saw it in terms of accomplishing the project, achieving the greater good. Ana should understand this with her loyalty to Essquibo. But then there was that basic difference between them, that inevitably different outlook when one's life was extended by half a millennium.

And Merv brought it up, Traci recalled. So, still another outlook then?

41.

The magnate rose from his chair and excused himself, saying he was going out for a smoke. He and his fellow clients had just heard the order in which they'd have surgery. He would be the first, which didn't surprise him, given that he was aggressive and had likely conveyed more enthusiasm. The others were a bubbly heiress, easily awed and talkative, and a South American rancher, suavely fatalistic.

Lighting his cigar, the magnate squinted at the numeral *1* on the door of the former model. His number, all right, but why was it on there? Another house well down the beach, he saw, then a small one far off. Two and three, perhaps? He shrugged and walked off toward the dock. An armed guard was standing on the pier scanning the water.

"Good evening," said the magnate.

"Good evening, sir."

"Lovely evening."

"Yes, sir. Excuse me."

The guard turned on his heel and strode away, taking a course along the line of trees above the cove. The magnate had a puff in isolation, considered going on toward the project, decided instead to explore down the beach path.

He came to number 14, puzzled over the number on the door.

"Well, I'll be," he muttered. "What does it mean?"

He saw a man lurking by the small house on the far end, the point. As the magnate began walking toward him, however, the man made his way inside and shut the door.

"What the hell," said the magnate. "Same to you, fella."

As he turned away, his gaze swept the cove, its opening to the sea directly across. It looked inviting after the rebuff from the point. Smiling at the notion, the magnate decided to wade in a bit. He shed his sandals and felt the fine sand caress his feet. The water, still warm, lapped about his ankles with a faraway sound. Faraway because it had been so long, he suddenly realized, since he'd done anything like this—simple, spontaneous, with real interest, heartfelt. For many years he might as well have been dead. But that would all be over soon, he thought. The emptiness would be filled. How he ached to have this treatment done with!

Some seabirds flew over. The magnate turned and twisted trying to follow their flight over the trees. His toes snagged something in the sand beneath the water. He bent and raised the object in the meager light. It was a swimmer's watch, waterproof. Flicking on his lighter, he saw that the watch was still running, its dials enclosed by a horseshoe inscribed *GOOD LUCK*. Turning the watch around, he saw the name inscribed on the back: *D. Tabor.*

"Well, Mr. or Ms. Tabor," said the magnate, "I don't mind having some luck in the mix on this thing. I'm readier than ever now!"

He pocketed the watch and headed back to shore. It had been a good walk after all, he decided. He anticipated success in this place, feeling as usual that he deserved it.

42.

The sky above Project Island was overcast, occasional drizzle sweeping in from the sea. Hans stood unperturbed atop the hill overlooking the heliport. Despite the weather, he thought, this day is beautiful. It was one of his rare stints as the man in charge, Dr. Kassander and others needing to rest from a marathon transplant operation. From all indications it'd gone well, but the assistants were taking turns sitting with the client, Hans checking with them on each rotation. The guards had been redeployed, guarding the dock against intrusive media and watching the cove as well. Hans didn't put it past the *paparazzi* to come in by outrigger or even as frogmen. He'd called a company contact to request doubling the guards, citing the operation, and was told it would happen tomorrow. Soon he'd make another call that would make guards even more necessary. In fact, checking his watch, he saw that it was time now.

Hans descended the hill, briefly considering how rain might affect the new guards' landing. It'll pass by then, he decided, and turned his thoughts to the more important matter. His part was rather simple, actually, but what followed would shake the world. Just a few facts, most of them mundane, recited to another contact. But one feature of the story would stun people, strike an innermost chord in everyone who heard it, the thought of which gave Hans a thrill, a sense of mastery over the world, over history. What more could any scientist—any man—want? Granted, he wasn't central to the achievement, but he was party to it and the one who was announcing salvation. He would deliver hope to mankind against its greatest fear.

After checking once more on the client, Hans hastened to his office to phone.

* * *

The article first appeared in the Internet edition of a European retirement magazine, in the medical news column. It was quickly picked up by news services for worldwide dispersal. The original article read:

ZURICH—Researchers from the Essquibo Institute have reportedly developed a process for extending the human lifespan by centuries. (!) According to a source within the Institute, a team of experts has been working on the project on a remote island in the Pacific Ocean. They have been led by Dr. Isador Kassander, an accomplished transplant surgeon, and Dr. Traci Spenser-Leeds, a controversial molecular biologist. The source emphasized that, while initial skepticism is expected, the Institute will soon release irrefutable evidence of their success. Further, the law firm of Thierry, Bates, and Welles has been retained to protect Essquibo's rights surrounding this discovery.

The report was embellished as the day wore on, reporters digging for background and citing supposed experts on life extension. Ethical issues and social implications were expounded. Skeptics delighted in scoffing, religious types in ranting. Behind the excitement, of course, was the overarching question: "What's in it for me?" People were cautioned by the sager commentators, however, to await the evidence and consider it carefully before making changes in their lives or beliefs.

"A tall order, that," said Phil in the commission chair's office. He'd come to see Dave at once on hearing the news. A small TV emanated follow-up.

"Yeah," Dave acknowledged. "It doesn't take much when people want to believe. And this isn't just flying saucers."

"What gets me is how close we were, Albert anyway, without even knowing. The power, the immense potential for profit, and we're next door trying to cut our losses."

"Gaville's, yeah, and their creditors."

"Think we'll catch flak for dumping it, the Cove of Dreams?"

Dave considered a moment, Phil twisting in his chair and frowning.

"Possibly. The value would've skyrocketed if we'd waited. But how could we have known? We weren't in the loop."

"Albert got involved in that deal to buy in with them, with Essquibo."

"Damn, that's right." A hesitation. "Well, don't worry about it. We have immunity from personal liability. You, me, Judge Richter. Just public officials performing in good faith. Untouchable."

"What about Albert?"

Dave made a steeple of his hands, stared at it.

"I know you go way back with him, but he's a case where we really do want to cut our losses. He'll be on his own on this. Around here, *persona non grata*. Sorry, Phil."

"No, Dave, that's all right. I understand."

Across the country, Mr. Ub sat with a glass of wine on the balcony of his condo. His wife had gone out alone when she saw he wasn't in the mood for shopping. Mr. Ub had considered a stronger drink but, feeling it was too early, decided a glass of wine would go nicely while reflecting on his folly. He should never have allied himself with that blowhard Groth, he thought. He should have had sufficient confidence in his commercial instincts, well honed after all, to approach the Essquibo man directly with his proposal. He'd shrunk from the bold course in favor of neurotic caution, conditioned by the insecurity of his tiny country. And for what? A position and ersatz status that he later abandoned anyway. Now, with the scale of Essquibo's prospects almost beyond comprehension, his retirement would proceed in the towering shadow of his failure. It was all so different from what he'd foreseen in emigrating.

The phone rang inside. He got up to answer it.

"Hello, old friend," came a familiar voice.

"Senator Rua?"

"We've missed you. People have come to appreciate you in your absence. We have need of your skills and wish you to return."

"Well, ah, I've retired. There was the letter I sent, the resignation."

"All that is immaterial now. With the big news, the fountain-of-youth story, our country stands to reap a bonanza. Project Island is within our border, so the Kingdom will be known as the country that nourished the miracle. We need you to help us capitalize."

Mr. Ub tried to compose himself, follow Rua's logic, evaluate it.

"I see what you mean," he said, "and I appreciate your offer, but of course we're all settled here and—"

"There's been a conference with the prince," Rua interrupted, "your former superior. He will vacate the post of trade minister once you accept it. A special promotion giving you full latitude to exploit our new identity, our windfall."

Mr. Ub was silent, confirming to himself that he'd heard right.

"So, what do you say?"

Across the ocean, much closer to the Kingdom and Project Island, another sort of opportunity was seen. In a small warehouse off a narrow crowded street, Fong listened skeptically to his son's latest proposal. Cartons of pharmacy goods surrounded them and there was a shipping setup in one corner. As Zing spoke in his enthusiastic way, Fong's brother and business partner came in and sat down.

"With the new name your business will take off," Zing was saying. "Think of it: 'Immortality Brand' on the packaging and labels, all your advertising, 'Developed on Project Island' right underneath it."

"That's all bogus," Fong objected. "Nobody will believe that."

"It's *not* bogus. You were working there the same time they were, thinking how to improve this business. So you developed the products there. And we can back it up with your personal story on a company website, with a link to order your products. And another even stronger slogan, something like 'Live for Centuries ' inside a starburst."

"Now, Zing," Fong began, but found he liked what he was hearing.

"You can add new products with a 'Cove of Dreams' angle, show there's more to the island than just Essquibo. Call it the 'Island of Health.' You can give interviews, be on TV health segments, maybe regular talk shows. Everywhere you go the company and the products get mentioned. Business will be booming."

Fong looked over at his brother, who nodded sagely.

"After a while," said Zing, "other guys will want your endorsement for *their* stuff "

* * *

As the overcast day grew darker, evening settling in, Hawkins made his way down the beach to check on the Hoorts' property. He'd thought of it earlier in the day, but the people from number 1 were out strolling and he wanted to avoid them. He'd seen the stories on the Internet and assumed these second and third clients would cause further waves of sensation. Very soon, of course, the waves would surge back, an unwelcome tide of scrutiny washing over his retirement retreat. He was increasingly bothered by the thought.

The locks on the Hoort house were secure, the golf cart parked in its accustomed spot. Standing by the house, Hawkins found that he missed the owners' company, and somehow Susanna more than Max. Whatever her flaws, he felt, she exuded a certain humanity, an endearing vulnerability, that distinguishes human beings in nature. The delicate intricacy of human life is what makes us respect it. The couple in number1, as well as the client recovering from surgery, sought to overcome their vulnerability. He himself had also, to a lesser extent. Essquibo sought huge profits from this, its employees places in history. Hawkins didn't blame anyone for wanting these things but felt hollow in the midst of it. He'd live an extra hundred years, right, but was it really such a big deal? Was it human? Maybe the human lifespan was its given length because it was truly all you needed. Plenty of time, plenty of life stages, for every worthwhile experience. Immortality might just be excess, repetition, stagnation.

It started to drizzle and Hawkins walked back to his cottage. He paused on the way to view the sea to the south. Low turbid waves sulked in the spray, shrouding the deathbed of Tabor and many others. The new procedure could not have stopped their deaths. There are boundaries for all creatures, limits to what even the superhuman can experience and survive.

He went in. It was time to dig out that business card, he thought, call Beau Jerome and see what he had to offer. Time to move on.

43.

Traci sat before the mirror in her small bedroom, brushing her abundant black hair. She stopped suddenly when she caught a certain look in her eyes, a look of disillusion, almost cynicism. She ran two fingers over the pale skin of her face, assuring herself she was the same as always, growing older with abnormal slowness. Standing, she ran her hands down the sides of her body, tracing the adolescent figure clad in flimsy underwear. Countless, infinite men would desire her, she knew, and yet the one she'd chosen to succeed Cyril was casually taking his leave. Granted, she'd had her own doubts about their future, that casualness of his wedded to her intensity, but it was hurtful anyway. A personal comedown, not quite humiliating but clearly less than what she deserved.

He'd dropped into the lab that day and asked to speak with her alone. Ana overheard and said she was about to leave anyway, something about the animals. Hawkins had been to see Hans, discussing his departure by helicopter, something he'd arranged himself with Essquibo. He said he was leaving for good the next day, and waited for Traci to react. But she was in her professional mode.

"We'll be sorry to see you go, I'm sure. All of us."

"I want you to know—about us, I mean—I'd like for things to go on, but—"

"No, I understand. With all that publicity, it won't be the same here. Maybe very hectic. I know that's not what you—well, not *for* you."

Hawkins was still contrite, visibly bothered. Traci felt rising sympathy for him, hoped she wouldn't cry.

"If you'd like to come by tonight," he said, "a farewell time together—"

She'd agreed with no real thought about it, a purely emotional reaction. It was to take away the scene in the lab, a personal awkwardness she hadn't felt in years. It was the only response within reach. Now, with the coming of night, his final one on the island, it was time to make good on her promise.

* * *

She wore a dark blue dress, midnight blue, instead of her usual lab coat. He seemed surprised by this but pleased, ushering her into the living room with some ceremony. He set out wine glasses and opened a fresh bottle. He asked if she'd like some music but she said no, the sound of the waves was fine. They were sitting apart, a certain formality having encroached on their relationship.

"Nice," she said, looking around and listening. "Sure you want to leave all this?"

"Right now, no. Not with you here and all."

"Mm, the world at peace. The far end of the earth, anyway."

"Yeah, the farthest end." He looked down reflectively. "That was my plan."

Traci studied him as she sipped. Had she interfered with this man?

"You know," she said, "I'm all right with what you're doing now, your moving. We had—well, we had our own plan more or less, but of course things change, things become more clear. We've both been through enough to know that."

Hawkins looked up and smiled.

"It's generous of you to say that. I appreciate it."

They sipped in silence a few moments. Once their eyes met, Traci gave a head tilt toward the bedroom.

"Want to go in there?"

He gave a look of pleasure but then peered into his wine. She made no move to get up, just sat back and observed him.

"It has to be 100 per cent between you and a woman, doesn't it? Otherwise, nothing much happens. True?"

"I'm sorry."

"No, it's okay. Because actually I'm that way, too. Ever since Cyril—well, except with you awhile—I just haven't been that interested. My passion has been the work."

Hawkins nodded but made no comment.

"How about a walk on the beach?" he asked instead. "We can bring the wine."

They carried their glasses, and Hawkins the bottle, as they left the cottage and trod the fine white sands of the cove. The night was partly clear, the moon half-full, with sporadic breezes rippling the water. Traci's hair lifted in the wind and she could feel her companion's glances, his admiration, perhaps regret. But neither of them said much until they reached number 14, turned up toward it, settled themselves on the porch with their wine. They were facing across the cove toward its outlet to the sea, to what lay beyond.

"Cove of Dreams," Traci mused. "Does that mean your dreams come true here, or it's a place you dream more than usual?"

"Intended as the former, no doubt," Hawkins replied. "In reality, the latter."

"I guess some people see value in that, just dreams by themselves."

"Yeah, I guess they do."

They were quiet awhile. Hawkins refilled their glasses.

"It's really fine sitting with you here," he said. "Having those plans, the feelings behind them, seems wild now, but I'm grateful for it, grateful to you for the experience. You lifted me out of my old crummy self. A little too high, maybe, but now we're fine, settled. We can see things as they are, be sane. Just demigods, not god and goddess."

"There's still the future, Merv. A long one for us."

"Yeah, that's right. I guess our paths could cross."

"Especially since we're both with Essquibo. 'Colleagues,' shall we say?"

Hawkins smiled and raised his glass.

"That's right. Here's to business."

* * *

In the end, Traci thought, there's never much to say. It's just action that brings finality. Hawkins had walked her through the trees, watched as she returned to the compound. She'd promised to be at the heliport next day when he departed. Now, as she returned to the residential unit, her small bedroom, she was aware of the need for one more action tonight, something to correct an imbalance she felt in her universe. It wasn't the relationship with Hawkins but something more fundamental, overarching. A basic assumption that ran through all she was doing here on Project Island. She had never doubted Cyril or his work, was willing to allow commercial exploitation to develop it, but perhaps she'd misjudged the resulting value of success right *now*, at this time and place. It could be that more thought should be given to what a person will *do* with added centuries of life, perhaps immortality.

She slipped out of the blue dress but didn't prepare for bed. Instead, she put on the spare lab coat she kept and went out again. It was late and no one was about; the guards were watching the coastlines.

Traci walked calmly yet purposefully to the synthesis lab. She used her key to enter and locked the door behind her. The dim security lights were on, creating a specter of secret activity appropriate for the hour. Cyril's notes were locked in their usual drawer; she'd decide later what to do with them. The computer was turned off for the night, Ana still following the project's original parsimonious protocol. Traci turned it on and sat at the console, brought up the heavily secured file on the chromosome. She wouldn't change much, just two or three minor details in the painstaking process of construction, maintenance, application. She'd have liked to alter Cyril's catalyst too, but Ana might know the formula from memory. Traci herself could remember the changes she was making now, if she wished.

She turned the computer back off when she'd finished, then braced herself for the hard part. It was as if Cyril were there with her—watching curiously, not comprehending.

"I have to do it," she said softly.

She went to the storage and containment area at the back of the lab, past the climate-control chambers to the rarely touched vials and arcane equipment. She spotted a container of EMS, ethyl methane sulphonate, and considered how she could use it. It would take very little to induce mutation, defeat the purpose of the chromosome, perhaps imbue negative effects. A small enough amount could be consumed in reaction, though what about a by-product or residue? There should be no sign of sabotage; the chromosome had to be seen as failing on its own, and responsible for any damage. But she needn't use a chemical mutagen, she knew. With a little more trouble, she could foil any analysis.

Traci walked back to the climate-control chambers and opened one that was locked, using the key pad beside the door. Inside there were seven vials, chromosomes in solution, two each for the new clients and Hawkins's left-over backup. They'd been constructed by exacting standards, resulting in the virtually perfect entities envisioned by Cyril. Immortality, even just from aging and disease, required perfection. A most delicate balance determined one's fate, both what you were and what happened to you.

She removed the vials and packed them in an insulated carrier. Without stopping for further thought, she left the synthesis lab with the carrier and proceeded to the EAU. She avoided any show of haste in case a guard spotted her. The animals were curious when she entered their night but she ignored them. She went back to the examining station opposite the mice cages and set down the carrier, keeping it clear of equipment she had to move. She swung down an X-ray apparatus and adjusted it, using a raised stage as if for a mouse. She turned the mechanism on. Unpacking the carrier, she moved the seven vials onto the stage in close rank. She took cover then, counted to three, and gave the vials a jolt. Some seconds passed, Traci not moving, then she hit the switch again. It was over.

Cautiously, lovingly, she returned the chromosomes to the synthesis lab, their climate-controlled chamber for ensuring stability. Tomorrow, after Hawkins left in his helicopter, the client with transplants would be infused from one of the vials. The second client on the island was scheduled for surgery that evening. Her donor would be Chastity, the female chimp, finally being allowed a role in the project.

Despite the late hour, Traci felt the need for a walk.

* * *

She stood on the hill above the heliport, watching the shifting clouds in the night sky, behind them the stars. Another 500 years, she thought, but of what? Perhaps she could do research on individual diseases. But what about her personal relationships? The others would be true mortals, 120 years at most, dying off through the centuries while she hardly aged. Would she have children, grandchildren, et cetera and watch them pass away while she herself lived on, regretting more and more what she was?

The tragedy of Cyril wasn't that he died or was wrong, but that humanity wasn't ready for his gift. People shouldn't have added life because it only brings pain unless something exists to balance it, a world friendly and fulfilling to them. We're not yet living in such a world. Cyril in his fervor didn't consider this, and one shouldn't try to save humanity unless he clearly sees what he's doing.

Some day things would be different, Traci thought. Civilization moves sluggishly on, irrational forces falling away in their rages. But for now, for her anyway, the manipulation of life and death was over. Except, it suddenly struck her, for herself. As she scanned the dark waves through which Tabor had his last swim, losing himself in the currents, she saw herself following him. She would just walk, though, and if she couldn't walk on water there would be one less goddess to confound humanity.

But no, she loved life too much. That's what she'd always been about.

She turned her back on the waves and descended to the compound, her waiting bed.

One more irrational force had fallen away.

EPILOGUE

After much thought and talking with a counselor, Leti Fong decided against pursuing medical studies. The pharmacy alternative suggested by her father did not appeal to Leti. She applied instead for admission to the university's business college. Since her grades were good but not outstanding, she needed to write a strong supplementary essay as part of her application. Her best bet, she decided, was to draw on the experiences of her father:

…my greatest influence, to whom I am most grateful and admire. He has always strongly supported my education and other needs, even at great and unusual hardship to himself. One may recall recent news stories about Essquibo, the project on an island out in the sea. My father did not work for them, but he worked for another company that shared that island with them. His employer was supposed to build vacation houses. They were very slow to get things going, so Father was almost alone most of the time, working hard so far away from family and friends. His only company was an older man who lived in a vacation house by himself. The Essquibo people stayed behind their fence with armed guards.

My father was there when some bodies washed up, when there were gunshots, when the police investigated the weird experiments. He did nothing to cause those things but he still had to deal with them, because the culprits were his neighbors. He says he was not surprised when the story came out about crossing people with apes and fake "immortality." He was mostly surprised that the doctors and their helpers didn't go to jail, and that some even got hired by universities. But Father and I are both aware that the laws and legal contracts must prevail, and that this can be very complicated when you are dealing with international incidents.

My father has also been partner right along with one of my uncles in a mail-order pharmacy business. Before the Essquibo project was a fiasco, my brother Zing thought Father should use his contact with it to publicize the pharmacy business. Father wisely declined, however, just using the name of the part of the island where he worked, the Cove of Dreams. Later he got the man he befriended there, Mr. Hawkins, to endorse Cove of Dreams products. Mr. Hawkins was known from the news shows for the information he gave about Essquibo. He was supposed to get a job from them but that dissolved with the aforementioned fiasco.

My father's experiences and resulting advice have been very valuable to me. I have come to recognize business studies as the avenue to a fulfilling career and my role in society. If admitted to your esteemed institution…

Leti submitted her application with the sense that she'd done all she could and would accept whatever fate wished to give her. The world seemed wild and unstable and she was happy just to live in a safe area with her family. But the university replied that Leti was accepted and with partial financial assistance. This was a great event for her father, who relayed the news to his friend Hawkins in America. Soon after, Leti received a congratulatory card with a monetary gift enclosed. It was signed "Lydia and Merv."

About the Author

James I. McGovern holds an M.A. in literature and has worked in education and human services in addition to writing. After some success with articles and short stories, he published several novels: *The Child Abuse Man* (1988), *Spring of Second Comings* (1993), *Aura of Purgatory* (2000), and *Beyond the Failure Club* (2007). A collection of his short fiction was published as *The Twin Fortunes and Other Stories* (2004). Mr. McGovern currently resides in northern Illinois.